HELL'S BELLES

CJ Walley

Copyright © 2024 CJ Walley

All rights reserved.

ISBN: 9798879510775

To the tomboys.

"The most effective way to do it, is to do it."
- Amelia Earhart

Chapter 1

Somewhere in the Middle East, sand carried by the wind sweeps across an empty highway.

A Humvee screeches up, and a Squad leap out. Some bad shit just went down.

They gather into a defensive formation while a Corporal shouts panicked into his radio, "This is Shortstack twenty-one requesting close air support on quadrant niner-six! Insurgents locked in tight, over!"

They exchange worried glances as they wait for a response.

"Received," the radio crackles. "Air support en-route to your area, Shortstack. Over and out."

They sigh, relieved.

A distant cackling in the distance causes them to all look toward the horizon.

A Blackhawk helicopter gunship skims the desert, a battered wreck going hell for leather and pouring out smoke from its massive jet turbines, on which 'Big Greasy' is crudely inscribed.

Taylor, tall, athletic, and cool as ice, sits slumped across the open side door, her hair blowing in the wind, the interior of Big Greasy shuddering like crazy.

Judge, an African-American woman, shoots Taylor a mean

stare from the cockpit.

"Put your damn lid on, Taylor!" Orders Judge.

"You know the enemy only shoot up at us, right?" Scoffs Taylor.

Judge ain't too impressed with that remark.

Spit, early-twenties, Latin-American, and just as alluring as that implies, straps in behind a mini-gun and jokes, "It's so, when your head explodes, we don't get covered in brains!"

Taylor pats her lid on, a pair of gonads scrawled on it. "You know I ain't got no brains!" She retorts.

Memphis, petite and sweet, clutches the control stick with a crazed stare in her eyes. "Comin' up on our ten-o-clock!" She warns.

Big Greasy storms over the squad, who gaze up to find The Girls grinning back and giving them the finger.

"Hell's Belles!" Exclaims The Corporal with fear in his eyes, "Retreat back!"

As Big Greasy approaches a ramshackle town, Memphis kisses her hand and taps a Pink Power Ranger toy glued to the dashboard.

The Girls intently scan the area as they circle it, scoping for a fight.

"There!" Signals Judge, "Nine-o-clock! Batter up!"

"On it like I wannit!" Replies Taylor, aiming her mini-gun with both hands and bracing herself.

BWAAAAAAAP!! A belt of ammo whizzes through the gun, as empty shells shower to the floor.

Insurgents get chewed into shreds in a hailstorm of bullets.

"On our five!" Barks Judge

Memphis cuts the stick with style, and Big Greasy kicks around.

It's Spit's turn with her mini-gun. BWAAAAAAAP!!

More insurgents are torn to pieces.

Then silence.

The girls sit waiting.

"That it?" Complains Judge. "They called us in for that boy-scout bullshit."

Spit lets out a disappointed sigh, "Tell me that was just the foreplay, please."

"Foreplay? That wasn't even third base," grumbles Memphis.

Taylor suddenly points forward. "Dead ahead!" She yells.

A beat-up old Pickup races out of a hiding place and skids to a halt with an RPG Weilding Insurgent in the bed.

He aims a rocket launcher at Big Greasy and fires.

Memphis puts the moves on him.

WOOSH! The rocket just misses and shrieks by, leaving a line of white smoke.

That Pickup is now getting out of town fast.

A devious grin forms on Judge's face. "Oh, now we're talkin'!" She shouts.

The Pickup flees down the streets.

Big Greasy swoops after.

Taylor and Spit clutch their mini-guns and open fire.

Dirt kicks up around the fleeing Pickup as rounds punch the ground and walls around it shatter.

It swerves down a street, but Big Greasy follows and looms over it.

RPG Insurgent fires back at the chopper.

BOOM! He misses again, and an old stone building takes the hit, debris flying everywhere.

They race into an industrial area and head for a huge warehouse.

The Pickup blows by a security booth and ducks through the open doors into the warehouse.

A Creepy Insurgent in the booth shouts, goads, and generally insults the concept of freedom as Big Greasy thumps by.

Judge looks worried. The warehouse doors approaching fast, filling the view out the windshield.

Memphis is in the zone, her eyes narrow. She's taking them in.

"Oh hell no," cries Judge, "Memphis! No!"

Big Greasy just manages to slip through the gap in the doors.

The Pickup races around stacked goods, tyres squealing on the concrete floor.

Big Greasy circles and fires, kicking up dust and blowing over objects, but The Pickup screeches down a passage and hides.

Silence. The Girl's pupils flick around, the shadow of the rotor blades strobing across them.

Insurgents everywhere, cleaning guns, playing cards, plotting bad guy shit.

They all freeze and stare back.

"Girls," Judge announces, "we are one big ass bull in one small ass china shop!"

Gunfire from pretty much everywhere.

Big Greasy spins round and round and unleashes hell, bullets sparking off its body.

The big warehouse doors slowly close shut, trapping them inside.

"Get us out of here, Memphis!" Orders Judge.

"No problem!" Assures Memphis with a smug smile.

Memphis waits until they spin back around to face the doors, flicks up her missile button, and fires.

WOOSH! A missile launches from Big Greasy, headed straight for the doors, but punches straight through them and rockets outside toward the security booth.

The creepy Insurgent in the booth goes wide-eyed.

BOOM! His booth explodes.

Memphis winces as she stares at the round hole of daylight in the door and asks, "Umm, anybody got any

4

better ideas?"

Spit's mini-gun suddenly cuts out. "I'm jammed!" She cries as she smacks the side of it.

Insurgents capitalize on it. They rush into positions and open fire.

Bullets ping against the body.

Memphis looks back. "Hang on!" She warns.

Big Greasy turns, sweeps back, and blows dirt into the Insurgent's eyes, but the tail crashes against an overhead walkway causing the tailwheel to get mangled into the framework.

The girls jolt. Memphis cringes as she fights the controls.

"What's the problem!" Taylor shouts, getting thrown around.

Memphis winces as she fights with the controls and can't get the tail free. "Shit! Now I'm jammed!" She yells.

Taylor's on it. She unbuckles, takes out her sidearm, crosses to Spit, and fires through the window, picking off Insurgents one by one.

Big Greasy writhes around, still caught on the walkway.

"Come on, Big Greasy!" Memphis urges, "Come on, baby!"

Big Greasy tilts right over to one side.

Taylor falls over, slides out of the side door on her back, drops through the air, and thuds to the warehouse floor.

She quickly leaps up, runs, and dives to cover behind crates and a forklift truck.

Judge pulls out her own pistol and fires from her window. "Could we be in any more of a mess!" She shouts.

"Yes!" Exclaims Memphis, her eyes widening as she stares ahead.

The girls snap around to see The Pickup has reappeared and RPG Insurgent is aiming right for them.

He surely can't miss this time, but then Taylor pops up from behind the crates and fires.

RPG Insurgent takes it in the leg. He buckles and fires.

WOOSH! The rocket shrieks past Big Greasy and hits the warehouse roof.

BOOM! The Squad who called them in, who've now retreated into the desert, wince as they peer into the distance and see a huge fireball erupting from the warehouse.

Memphis glances around. An Insurgent on the walkway, crossing toward the tail.

She kicks the rudder hard, and the tail rotor screams as it speeds up, the force sucking the Insurgent into the rotors and chopping him to shreds.

Taylor defends her position, but her pistol is rapidly running out of ammo.

She pauses, looks down, and notices something.

Turns out the crates around her are full of AK47s!

She grabs one, unloads a whole clip into insurgents, grabs another, and repeats.

Spit manages to unjam her gun. "I'm back!" She announces as she lets rip and cuts into the stuck tailwheel.

Taylor grabs another AK and gets on the forklift.

She races across the warehouse and raises the ammo crate while firing back at insurgents.

She jams the AK on the throttle, climbs up the lift, leaps to Big Greasy, and straps back in behind her mini-gun like it's another tough day at the office.

"Good to finally have you back with us, Taylor!" Commends Judge, "Now let's get the hell out of here!"

Taylor nods sagely out the window. "Gladly!" She replies.

She aims for something and opens up her mini-gun.

BWAAAAAAAP!! A huge rack of fuel barrels cuts apart and collapses, causing the barrels to clang to the floor and roll along as the Forklift bumbles toward them.

The Pickup screeches out from its hiding place and dives outside through a gap in the door.

Judge aims her pistol carefully, squints, and fires.

BOOM! The ammo crate on the Forklift explodes, blowing up fuel barrels with it.

The Pickup races away from the exploding warehouse as the wall blasts apart behind it.

The girls shield themselves as Judge screams, "Motherfuckers, we are a weapon of mass destruction!"

Spit continues firing.

The tailwheel breaks free.

Big Greasy pulls away through an onslaught of exploding barrels and storms out of the collapsing warehouse before diving toward the highway in pursuit of the Pickup.

Two Motocross bikes take chase while the building explodes behind them in a huge orange fireball.

The Squad in the desert all nod, whoop, and applaud.

Big Greasy chases the Pickup, ducking under an overpass like it's routine, with the bikes on its tail.

The bikes get in close behind. The pillion riders fire. Bullets ping.

Memphis pulls back on the stick and screams, "HOLD ONTO YOUR TITS!"

Big Greasy pitches back and smacks an overhead sign, causing it to crash down to the asphalt.

One bike smacks into the twisted metal and throws off the riders, while the other ramps it and continues firing.

"Enough of this!" Orders Judge, "Belle Break!"

The girls all clutch on. They know what's coming.

Big Greasy kicks back, rolls, and spirals up and around the bike in one insane death-defying move.

The Squad stare, shocked, as their heads follow the seemingly out-of-control chopper.

"Where the hell they learn that?" Wonders a Squad Member, his eyes wide.

"They invented that shit," replies another.

Big Greasy swoops down and smacks the bike over.

The Insurgent riding pillion flies through the air and

disappears under Big Greasy.

Memphis and Judge search around for him to find he's now hanging from the landing gear, fear in his eyes as asphalt rushes by.

Big Greasy hugs the road, flies completely sideways, and draws alongside the Pickup.

The Driver and RPG Insurgent stare in shock. The Insurgent clinging to the landing gear shrugs back.

Judge snatches up a microphone.

"You in the truck, pull over!" She barks through the PA system.

The Driver can't believe what he's hearing.

RPG Insurgent still fancies his chances. He grabs a rocket and goes to reload.

The girls shake their heads. Yeah, that ain't gonna happen.

BWAAAAAAAAAAAAAP! Both Big Greasy's mini-guns light up, and hell is unleashed on the pickup.

WOOSH! BOOM! A missile shrieks and detonates.

The burning pickup shell flips down the highway.

Big Greasy banks, turns, and victoriously soars away.

The girls celebrate by smacking in high-fives.

Taylor slumps down, takes off her helmet, and holds it up to find a bullet impaled into it.

Judge shakes her head, unimpressed.

Memphis proudly pats the Pink Power Ranger.

The Squad stare fixed as thick black smoke pours from the scene of destruction ahead and fills the sky.

The Corporal takes in the carnage and solemnly shakes his head. "You know what they say about Hell's Belles, boys," he concludes, "hell hath no fury like a woman scorned."

Big Greasy thunders over them, and the one remaining Insurgent crashes to the ground by his feet.

Job done.

* * *

A Captain enters an army meeting room at night, concern written across his face, while an Officer and an Advisor sit obediently waiting.

"So... Hell's Belles." He sighs as he takes a seat at the table.

"Hell's Belles," echoes the Advisor, rolling her eyes.

"Hell's Belles," repeats the Officer, shaking his head.

The Captain sits down, and they all open their files.

Elsewhere on the base, The Girls mosey through the darkness past campfires. They're cool, they're mean, and they look like trouble.

They head for a tent decorated with flashing fairy lights, a beat throbbing from within it.

Inside, Troops drink and dance. One hell of a party going down.

"Okay, tell me about these girls." The Captain orders as he studies his file.

A concerned Soldier from the party tent rushes up. He really doesn't want The Girls joining in.

Judge glares, gestures, and points at him as she confidently shouts back.

"Colonel Judith Newton, aka 'Judge Judy'," explains The Officer, "Left a high-power career as a lawyer in Baltimore following a messy divorce. She's got an eye for detail and a nose for bullshit, knows every rule, every loophole, every clause in our procedures and uses it to get whatever she wants."

Judge stands victorious outside the party tent, the Soldier reluctantly letting The Girls enter.

"And that's without ever playing the sexism or racism cards," adds The Advisor.

"Certified man-hater," The Officer continues, "she's got zero respect for men in unfair positions of authority and loves to challenge them."

"But, that's most of us here?" Exclaims the Captain.

"Doesn't seem to put her off, sir."

The Captain goes back to his files. "Okay, who else?"

Spit struts confidently toward a dance area. Lights flash, and colored laser beams flicker while sweat-covered bodies gyrate.

"Valentina Armero," explains The Advisor, "or as she's fondly known, 'Spit-Roast'."

The beat builds in the party tent, and Spit slips into the dancing crowd. She's sexy, and she knows it.

"Spit-Roast? Why the nickname?" Asks the Captain.

The Advisor winces back. "Really? Do I need to draw you a diagram?"

"Father emigrated from Columbia," adds The Officer, referencing his notes, "signed up first thing. She's Force through and through, knows nothing else."

"Other than how to sleep her way through most of her barracks," adds The Advisor, "she's a slut."

"I think the term is 'nymphomaniac'," corrects The Captain.

Spit seductively entwines with a Soldier and grinds against him.

"Oh no," exclaims The Advisor, "she's what nymphomaniacs call a slut."

"She's the one we want to protect," advises The Officer, "the others are a bad influence."

The Captain stares back dumbfounded. "She's the good one?" He exclaims.

Tiny Memphis stands lonely within the heaving crowd as she sips a beer and chews her lip, her pupils flicking around, paranoid

The Advisor opens Memphis' file. "Isabella Amesbury aka 'Memphis Bella', wanted to join so bad she ran away from wealthy parents in Beverly Hills at fifteen and tried to enrol."

Mephis jolts as she's accidentally shoved and flips out.

She coils and points venomously up at the Soldiers towering over her like a cornered street cat facing a pack of dogs.

"Tiny, neurotic and full of anger," lists The Officer, "she's a tempestuous little c-."

"-Ah ah ah!" interjects The Captain, "This room does not want to hear your personal opinion or that tone."

"No, sir," The Officer replies, holding up a report scrawled with red profanities, "her psychologist's words."

Memphis fearlessly launches into the Soldiers and starts swinging punches.

"After she broke his nose," adds The Advisor.

The Captain massages his temples for a moment before moving on to the next file. "Okay, so what about this last one, Taylor Trashmann?" He asks.

Taylor chugs her beer as she watches Memphis scrapping. She shakes her head, tosses the bottle down, and moves in.

"Taylor Trash," jokes The Officer.

"You say that to her face," challenges The Advisor, "She's six foot of pure go fuck yourself."

Taylor crosses to the brawl, pulls Memphis out by the scruff of her neck, and squares up to everybody.

"Raised in the deep South," details The Officer, "childhood so screwed up she entered kindergarten with a thousand-yard stare."

A soldier gets in Taylor's face. CRACK! She head-butts him and knocks him out.

The Captain slams the folder shut and slides it away from him. "Okay, skip to the chase for me here. What's the big issue?" He asks.

"They're a good crew," summarises The Advisor, "just too aggressive."

A full-blown fight breaks out in the party tent, Taylor swinging haymakers at everyone.

The Officer leans in with a frank look and explains, "They

cause too many problems both on and off the battlefield."

Spit and Judge run in and try to restrain Taylor, but Memphis leaps from a table back into the mix and makes things even worse.

"Put it this way, sir," concludes The Advisor, "they're so volatile, sometimes we'd be safer if they were fighting for the other side."

The Captain sits back and thinks.

The next day, on the Army Base, Big Greasy sits dumped on its damaged tail in the dirt, riddled with bullet holes, with Memphis in the cockpit, doing routine checks.

Spit catches some rays on a camp bed in a bikini while Taylor applies new skin to her knuckles.

Judge marches out of a tent with a radio to her ear, taking no shit. "Hell no!" She barks. "You tell your captain I want maintenance out here stat. No more bullshit!… Yeah, well, go get him. I'll tell him what the procedure is."

Crunching footsteps. Judge looks around.

The Advisor and Officer stood side by side, looking serious.

"Colonel," requests The Advisor, "a word please."

Judge sighs. The Girls exchange concerned glances.

They clearly ain't here to give them a badge of honor.

A few hours later, with the tent surrounded by darkness, The girls sit perched on their beds, shocked and angry.

Judge looks guilty, as if she's just delivered some bad news.

"Cargo crew?" Exclaims Spit, "Are you joking us? "

"Don't lay this at my feet," argues Judge, "I fought our case, but we just done too much stupid shit."

"Flying vans?" Questions Memphis, "Seriously? That's all we're good for? The Army's freaking delivery service?"

Judge waves her finger, "Hey, it's an essential role! Don't

demean it!" She states.

"She's right, though," grumbles Taylor, folding her arms tightly, "We're fighters, and we get the job done."

Judge shakes her head. "Not the way they want it done, we don't," she explains, "We break too many rules, we take too many risks, it's as simple as that."

"No!" Snaps Taylor, "It's called war, and it's as simple as us or them. These pencil pushers need to come for a ride-along, put some real lead down on the enemy, see how long they stick to procedure then."

"That's right!" Agrees Spit, "I just want to fight for something good, you know? My rules. I'll take my own risks."

They all look down and sigh while Memphis storms out furious and yells, "This is bullshit! Bullshit!"

A dusty makeshift airbase in the middle of nowhere. Rock music crackles through tannoy speakers.

Cargo Crew work hard with The Girls in their separate work areas; Taylor heaves crates. Spit stacks boxes. Judge scans paperwork.

Inside the control tower, Chad Man, an all-around weapons-grade douchebag, sits alone, slumped in his chair while slurping a soda and broadcasting into a mic, "And that was, of course, Beach Boys with Good Vibrations," he drones, "This is Chad Man The Bad Man, bringing a refreshing breeze of cool to your otherwise short and pointless existence as we slowly grind our way toward our inevitable demise at the hands of our enemy. Now, a little something for you ladies."

Spit and a Female Co-Worker roll their eyes as they listen to him through the tannoy.

"So all you honeys just lie back," he continues, "think of your country, and let the Chad Man slip into every orifice."

The Co-Worker pretends to gag on her finger. Spit smirks.

Chad Man puts the mic by a Boom Box speaker as cheesy R&B plays and spots a Cargo Plane coming in to land.

"Yo! Big wassup four fan trash can," he calls into the radio, "I've eye'd you in the sky, now please, identify."

A female voice crackles through the speaker, "This is Memphis coming in South for touchdown."

A sly grin draws across Chad Man's face. "Well, well, well," he replies, "the Chad Man and Memphis mouth to mouth once again!"

Inside the cargo plane, at the controls, Memphis is not happy to hear his voice.

Chad Man licks his lips and flicks a few switches. "You still aching for the Chad Man?" He asks.

Feedback squeaks through the tannoy speakers before the conversation is broadcast throughout the base.

"You still pining from the best night of your life?" He continues.

"Whatever, Chad Man!" Barks Memphis, "Screw you!"

Judge snaps up from her documents. This is worrying. Crew chuckle, amused.

Chad Man grins, his eyes darting around. "Screw me? Again?" He taunts, "In your dreams, baby. In your WILDEST dreams."

He peers at the runway with a smug smile as the Cargo Plane lands below.

Taylor stops work and listens. She knows where this is going.

"The Chad Man doesn't do seconds, cutie pie," he mocks, "It don't matter how many love letters you write in."

Spit stops stacking boxes and looks up concerned at the tannoy speakers.

"Fuck you Chad! Go to Hell!" Shouts Memphis.

Tires screech. Spit snaps around to see The Cargo Plane skidding to a halt, smoke pouring from the landing gear.

Memphis flicks overhead switches, getting really pissed

off.

The loading ramp whirrs down as Crew rush in to unload.

Memphis sneers into her radio. "You know what, Chad? You're a jerk!" She says. "A real dick dipping jerk! You know that, asshole!"

Crew snigger as Taylor grows really concerned.

Judge is now at the foot of the Control Tower, waving her arms for Chad Man to cut it out, but there's no chance. He's the Chad Man, and he loves the attention.

"Jerk, yeah?" Questions Chad Man, "That's not what you were saying a few weeks back."

Chad Man takes out his cell phone and flips it open to read from it.

Crew busily unload the Cargo Plane as the conversation continues to be broadcast in public.

"Message three-hundred-and-twenty four of eight-hundred-and-sixty-two;" he reads out, "Chad man, you bad man-"

Memphis is horrified, her broken heart still tender. "Don't you dare, Chad!" She threatens, "That poem's private!"

Crew wince. He's going too far.

Spit's getting worried. Taylor's getting anxious. Judge paces around.

Chad Man continues, "You make me sad, man. I'm mad, man."

He pauses and snorts, "Yeah, you're crazy! Like that's news to anybody!"

Memphis just got that crazy switch flicked. "Seriously," she screams, "don't call me crazy!"

She thrusts the power levers and adjusts the pitch. The engines roar at full speed. Crew flee.

The Cargo Plane starts backing up.

Judge freezes. Spit's eyes go wide. Taylor winces.

Shit just got crazy, and it's at the helm of a Cargo Plane.

Memphis grits her teeth, clutching the control stick tightly.

Chad Man peers at the runway, confused to see the Cargo Plane reversing down it fast.

"Umm," Chad Man informs. "I have not given you permission to race backwards down my airstrip, Memphis."

Taylor stares, watching the Cargo Plane charging backwards as Crew run for their lives. She knows it's only going to get more stupid.

She climbs up on a crate, scans the area, and spots Spit before gesturing a steering wheel.

Spit ain't too sure they should, but Taylor pleads, and Spit reluctantly gives in, running to a Humvee, firing it up, and racing away.

The Cargo Plane stops reversing suddenly, causing it to pop a little wheelie and crash back down.

Judge needs to get in that Control Tower and stop this. She runs to the ladder, but a Guard blocks her.

"Let me up there," she demands, "or we're gonna have one hell of a situation here!"

The Guard shakes his head sternly and assures, "No chance, sweetheart! Back off!"

Spit skids to a halt in the Humvee by Taylor, and she leaps in.

It scrabbles away toward the airstrip, but Memphis rams her power levers forward again, eyes glaring, and the Cargo Plane roars down the asphalt.

The Humvee crashes through a wire fence, racing after it, and drawing alongside the loading ramp.

Taylor leaps and grabs the ramp as the Cargo Plane pulls up sharply.

She hangs on tight as the ground sweeps away below.

Memphis shoves the control stick forward, and the Cargo Plane levels off fast, causing her to float up in her seat from the negative g-force.

Taylor smacks against the ramp and winces.

She looks up to find a Humvee jostling around in the

cargo bay, only partly secured.

"Directive forty-two!" Judge details to The Guard at the bottom of the Control Tower, "In the interest of base safety, security should show leniency-"

"Listen!" He barks, "There ain't nothing in that head of yours that's going to get you in this control tower!"

Judge looks back frankly for a moment. "Ya think?" She asks.

SMACK! She head-butts him, knocking him out, and then clutches her head while wincing.

"Shit! Ow! How does Taylor do that?" She exclaims.

Spit gazes up into the sky, watching the carnage unfolding above.

Chad Man is terrified, and he should be.

The Cargo Plane banks tight and levels off, coming right at the control tower fast.

"Hey now! It's cool!" He whimpers into the radio, " I'm just having a little fun, is all! I'm sorry! What we had was special, okay? Real, real special to me!"

Memphis stares ahead as The Tower closes in fast.

"Yeah? You promise?" She asks.

The Cargo Crew smirk as they listen to the tannoys. Chad Man's such a pussy.

"Yeah, I promise, honey!" He squeals, "I promise!"

"Well, okay then!" Accepts Memphis.

She pulls the control stick back hard, and the Cargo Plane pulls up at the last second.

Judge clutches onto the Control Tower ladder, her eyes clenched shut.

Chad Man screams like a girl and cowers.

The belly of the Cargo Plane fills the Control Tower window, and it just misses, pulling into a steep climb.

Crew applaud.

Taylor clings on for her life as the Cargo Plane goes vertical, the Humvee above her hanging by a single strap.

Memphis sits pressed back in her seat like an astronaut in a rocket. "Chad, now we're like, cool again," she says.

Chad Man's cowers on the floor, confused and scared. "Yeah, sweetie. We're cool," he confirms.

Taylor's eyes bulge. The strap holding the Humvee splaying apart, thread by thread.

Memphis smiles to herself. "How about I give you a hummer?" She offers.

Chad Man grins. A hummer? After this? Oh, hang on.

The strap suddenly snaps. The Humvee drops like a stone.

Taylor lets go of the ramp, drops, crabs a cargo net, and swings out of the way as the Humvee soars right by her.

The Humvee tumbles through the sky for a few beautiful seconds and impales into the Control Tower roof.

Crew fall about laughing. They can't believe it.

Chad Man lies coughing on the floor within a mess of ceiling tiles and structural beams around him. He eases his eyes open to find The Humvee grill staring back.

The door to the room slams.

He around to find Judge standing over him, shaking her head.

"See what you done?" She states.

He looks up helplessly as she snatches his headset off him and talks into it. "Memphis, you receiving?" She asks.

"Judge? Is that you?" Replies Memphis.

"Yeah, it's me. It's all cool, okay."

"You in air traffic control now?"

The click of a pistol. Judge winces and looks around to find The Guard with his gun raised, pissed off and nursing his bruised forehead.

"Not for long, baby," informs Judge, "I need you to put that bird on the ground right away, okay?"

"No problem!" Chirps Memphis before shoving the control stick forward and sending the Cargo Plane into a steep dive.

Taylor hangs onto the net, now flying in mid-air.

The Cargo Plane lands hard on the dirt near the airstrip and Taylor smacks into the ground, dragging along behind and wincing until the Cargo Plane skids to a halt in a cloud of dust.

Spit sighs, relieved it's over as sirens draw closer.

Military Police race up, and she raises her hands slowly.

Memphis goes to exit out the back of the Cargo Plane to find Taylor marching up the cargo area, filthy and furious.

Memphis freezes, and Taylor smacks her to the ground, pointing venomously as she hisses, "You really, really need to address your serious aggression issues!"

Judge looks down at the floor and cringes as Chad Man winces back, ashamed.

She raises the microphone to her mouth and informs the whole base, "Let the record show, Chad Man, 'The Bad Man', has managed to piss his pants."

As that final note echoes around the tannoy system, Crew fall about laughing and pointing at the Humvee wedged into the Control Tower.

Best day on base ever.

Inside an empty hanger, The Captain marches past The Girls lined up in front of him, with the Officer and Advisor standing obediently on either end of the line. He's seething,

He pauses by Spit. "Taking a vehicle without permission," he lists, "Invading the confines of a military air base."

Spit hangs her head in shame.

He pauses by Judge. "Assaulting a security officer," he continues, "Commandeering control of an aircraft."

Judge bites her lip, frustrated.

He pauses by Taylor. "Boarding a vehicle without orders," he continues again, "Boarding an aircraft without orders."

Taylor shakes her head, sneering.

He pauses by Memphis, looks her up and down, and shakes his head before concluding, "Pretty much everything else."

Memphis stares at the floor, angry.

He crosses to the center of the hanger in front of them.

"Sir," argues Judge, "let me just-"

"Shut your mouth, okay?" Barks The Captain, "Objection overruled, Ally-Mc-Fucking-Beal! Let me paint the picture for you here. I've now got a situation so densely fucked up it's actually now gathering mass! And if I don't do something, it's going to start sucking in more fucked up situations from the immediate vicinity, until this whole division becomes some sort of bullshit blackhole!"

He glares across at them all as they shamefully stare back.

"But I looked into you girls," he continues, his tone softening, "your mission reports, everything, and I get it. You take me back to a time when we stuck with our crew like shit on a shoe, and we got the job done, even if it meant breaking a few rules. Now maybe I'm getting all misty-eyed, or going soft in my old age, and believe me, my hands are pretty fucking tied here, but I'm throwing you a lifeline. You're disenrolled pending review. You fly back to the stars and bars with immediate effect."

The girls sigh, disappointed, and shake their heads.

"So go paint your nails," he advises, "braid each other's hair, sing some karaoke, or whatever it takes for you all to find some inner fucking zen. Dismissed!"

Back outside their tent, Memphis gazes ahead solemnly as she strokes the nose of Big Greasy.

Taylor and Spit exit the tent concerned.

"Memphis, it's going be okay," assures Taylor, "Don't worry about it."

Memphis nods forlornly as Taylor outstretches her arms.

"Come on," encourages Taylor, "bring it in."

Memphis trudges over and embraces her. Spit wraps her arms around both of them.

Judge pops her head out of the tent and beams.

"There's my girls," she cheers before joining the group hug.

They all clutch onto one another tightly.

Memphis starts to cry and whimpers, "I just always want to be with, you guys, you know. Seriously, I don't want us to be split up ever."

Judge's eyes glisten, it's all very emotional. "Quit it," she grumbles, "you're starting me off."

Spit sniffs, upset, and tries to laugh it off. "They can't keep the Hell's Belles apart for forever, yeah?" She states.

Taylor turns away and hides her tears before concluding, "You pussies really need to man up."

A few days later, The Girls slouch in the shuddering hold of a transport plane, the engines droning through the fuselage.

"I mean, I just don't get it, you know?" Worries Taylor, "What the hell am I going to do? Get a job? All I'm good at is shooting guns and punching people."

She thinks for a moment and shrugs. "Maybe it's time to find a good guy, settle down, make babies." She wonders.

"Seriously!" Exclaims Memphis with delight, "You think it's time?"

Taylor shoots back a dour look, and Memphis finally gets the sarcasm.

"You're lucky," advises Spit, "At least you've lived on the outside. What kind of job can I expect? Housemaid for some lazy rich guero?"

Memphis thinks for a moment. "I could ask my parents," she offers, "see if they'll give you jobs."

"Yeah?" Asks Spit, "What's their business?"

"A funeral home. It's good work. I like it. It would just be good if, like, some of the people there could talk back, you know?"

Spit's cringe says it all, and Memphis winces deflated.

"I don't know how to do anything else," explains Memphis, "seriously, I never finished junior high, and I'm pretty sure watching Saved By The Bell every day for three years doesn't count as homeschooling."

"Yeah," agrees Taylor, "that only counts if you've watched The College Years."

Judge lets out a deep, long sigh.

Spit rubs her knee to comfort her. "Why you so worried, Judge?" She questions, "You can just go back to law, eh?"

"You think?" Laughs Judge, "Oh, when I left, I did not go gracefully. I made sure EVERYBODY knew what I thought. No, I'm just as screwed as Morticia Adams and Kid Rock here, and, for what it's worth, I've been married. I joined the force to relax from that shit."

They glumly look at one another for a few moments.

"So..." ponders Taylor, "you guys wanna, like, stick together when we get to L.A? I mean, who knows when this review will come up. No point getting too settled down, right?"

They exchange nods, but then they don't need much of an excuse to stay together.

Memphis smiles, delighted.

Chapter 2

The L.A. skyline glints in the sun as traffic clogs highways. The Hollywood sign stands proud in the hills while surfers ride waves toward the beaches.

A massively oversized black Pickup Truck towers above bustling traffic as it cruises along.

Rap music booms. The Pink Power Ranger wobbles on the dash.

Memphis drives while singing along to the radio, scooched right up behind the wheel, with Taylor singing from the passenger seat.

They pull up at a set of lights and dance around, throwing goofy gang signs and poses.

Something catches Memphis' eye.

Gangsters glare up from an SUV pulled up beside them.

She stares back, unfazed. "What do these guys think they're staring at?" She scoffs.

Memphis continues her deadeye.

A Gangster briefly flashes a Beretta.

She drops her jaw sarcastically, unzips her hoody, and flashes a Glock.

Taylor clips her round the ear and exclaims, "Hey! It's called concealed carry for a reason. Conceal it."

"They won't shoot a little girl," argues Memphis.

"They will. They'll shoot you in the tits. That's what they do to girls. I saw it on The Wire."

"Shoot on my tits?"

"Yeah, sure. They're gonna get out of their car, drag you into the street, and shoot on your tits. Make a real example of you."

"Where's Spit when you need someone to take one for the team, right?"

"Just tell her there's a gang bang in town, she'll come running."

They laugh and roar away as the signal turns green.

Outside a cheap motel, Judge and Spit stand waiting on the sidewalk, dressed smartly with their luggage while checking their watches.

"Finally!" Calls out Spit as she spots The Pickup cruise by with Memphis and Taylor grinning back from inside.

Judge rolls her eyes at the oversized monstrosity blowing smoke from its stacks. "Is she driving that thing because she lost a bet?" she exclaims, "All she needs is a damn farm animal in the back."

"Why?" Questions Spit, "She's got one in the passenger seat."

Taylor smirks at Judge and Spit as they pull up to them.

"Does Judge think we're going to church?" She jokes.

Memphis glances in her mirror at Judge struggling to lift her luggage into the truck bed and jokes, "Judge religious? Seriously, taking orders from a man?"

The rear doors open. Spit climbs up and inside effortlessly, but Judge huffs and puffs as she tries to scrabble up in her pencil skirt.

"For crying out loud!" Rants Judge as she writhes away hopelessly, legs peddling in midair.

Taylor and Memphis laugh as Spit drags Judge up into her seat.

Judge slams the door, frustrated, and continues ranting, "How'd you even get in this thing, Memphis? You use a step ladder?"

"She wears appropriate clothing," replies Taylor.

Judge looks them up and down. "Oh yeah?" She says, "You two ever thought about trying to give a good first impression? Look at you, dressed like you're going to a damn sophomore football game."

Taylor rolls her eyes. "It's concert security, Judge," she reminds her, "We're not applying for jobs at Microsoft."

Spit leans in to check herself in the rearview mirror and straightens up her blouse. "My father, when I was little, he always told me, dress for the job you want, not the job you have," she says.

"Yeah?" Questions Taylor, "In that case, why aren't you dressed as a hooker?"

A little later, The Pickup cruises along the busy open highway toward the mountains.

Judge peers around and studies a map. "Why are we still on the damn interstate?" She asks.

Memphis glances at the GPS. "Umm, because, like, that's what the GPS says?" She replies, "Seriously, what's the problem?"

"The problem is your computer is sending us East. We need to be headed South."

Memphis and Taylor exchange eye rolls.

"I think the GPS knows best, Judge," says Taylor.

"Like hell it does!" Barks Judge, "I didn't spend years training to have some jumped-up smartphone with a suction pad tell me which way to go! No, come off at the next exit, I got this."

"No, don't," urges Taylor.

"Excuse me?" Asks Judge, "Did somebody get a promotion I didn't hear about?"

"You can't pull rank now, Judge," complains Memphis, "seriously, you can't boss us around out here."

"Oh, I'm not saying I outrank you," states Judge, "I'm simply stating I outclass you, okay? I outsmart you, I outperform you. Now I found these jobs, I got us these interviews, I planned this weekend, this is my thing, so what I say goes. And why am I all cramped up in the backseat anyhow? Why is Taylor up front?"

"Because I'm the tallest!" Reasons Taylor.

"Oh, is that how it works?" Questions Judge, "I try to get your sorry asses a job, and you throw it all back in my face, turn up dressed like idiots, make us all late, make me ride in the back?"

Taylor shakes her head, defeated, and sighs, "Fine! You know what, pull over!"

The Pickup quickly pulls over to the side of the road and stops.

Taylor and Judge both get out and storm around to each other's sides, their feet kicking up dust.

Everyone patiently waits while Judge, once again, huffs and puffs her way up into her seat.

Eventually, they get back on their way as Judge studies her map.

"There's more room back here!" Exclaims Taylor as she gestures at Memphis, "She has her seat so far forward I could give birth! In a birthing pool!"

Judge completely ignores her and scans the area. "Okay, now we're cooking," she says, "Take this exit up ahead."

A little later again, The Pickup drones along an empty desert road in what genuinely appears to be the middle of bumfuck nowhere.

Spit tries to get comfortable in her seat and looks across to find Taylor staring back, bored.

"What?" Asks Spit.

"I wish I was Mexican," states Taylor.

Spit turns away and leans against her window, watching the odd cactus pass by.

"Seriously," continues Taylor, "being Mexican is sexy."

"She's Columbian," states Judge, "not Mexican, Taylor."

Taylor winces, not understanding. "Same thing, right? Pretty much?" She questions.

Spit turns back to her, frustrated, and asks, "Why do you always have to take the piss out of my culture?"

"Well, I was tryin' to show an interest," exclaims Taylor, "Jeeze! Sorry!"

Taylor crosses her arms while sulking and glances at Spit.

"What?" Asks Spit, now really pissed off.

"Teach me some Spanish," requests Taylor.

"Like what Spanish?"

"Like, say I've just pounded some taco bender at a concert for, I dunno, pouring a forty on someone. What would be a cool thing to say?"

Spit sighs to herself, "Como Chingas."

"Yeah, like that," encourages Taylor, "that sounds cool."

"You want a good phrase?"

Taylor nods keenly.

"Okay," agrees Spit, "you repeat after me. 'Chupa'."

"Chupa."

"'Mi.'"

"Mi."

"'Polla'."

"Polla."

"'Chupa mi polla'."

"Chupa mi polla." *(Translation: 'Suck my Dick.')*

"What does it mean?" Asks Taylor.

"It's like, kiss my ass," assures Spit, "but way more badass."

Taylor nods, impressed, as Spit leans back content.

"Chupa mi polla," rehearses Taylor, "oh, you can chupa

mi polla, asshole."

Even later again, on yet another seemingly endless desert road, The Pickup pulls up to a halt.

The wind whistles. Birds of prey shriek.

Silence. The girls slouched, fed up.

Judge peers around, confused, and checks the map over and over.

"Admit it," says Taylor, "you're lost."

"How much longer?" Demands Spit, "I gotta pee."

Judge folds down the map. "Where's that GPS think we at?" She asks.

Memphis nods to the screen. "Knock yourself out."

Judge looks at the GPS to find it displaying the message *FIND NEAREST ROAD*.

Spit spots a car approaching. "We should ask for directions, yeah?" She asks.

"Look, I got this, okay?" Assures Judge, "We don't need to be asking around for help."

Spit writhes in her seat. "Come on," she urges, "if I don't pee soon, this big ass truck is going to be one wet ass truck!"

Memphis snaps, "Spit, seriously, if you pee in my truck, I will make you ride in the bed, okay?"

A battered and dusty old black 80's Firebird slows down and creeps by.

Pancho, a cool, handsome Mexican, stares up from the passenger seat.

Memphis gives him the finger. "Take a picture, Knight Rider," she grumbles.

"Chingalo!" Yells Spit as she gets out in a hurry.

Spit runs from the Pickup and waves her arms for help. "Hey! Hey!" She cries out.

The Firebird stops, engages reverse, and slowly backs up to her.

Pancho smiles back from inside, a guy beside him at the

wheel, and a teenage Mexican Girl in the back.

"You got car trouble?" Asks Pancho.

Oh no, we're just lost out here," explains Spit.

He shakes his head, amused. "What is it with girls and getting lost, man?" He wonders, "Why can you not find your way around for shit?"

Spit politely laughs along.

"Your friend," continues Pancho, "she gave me the finger. She got a real attitude problem."

"Oh, that," dismisses Spit, "it's nothin'. She's in a lot of therapy, you know?"

Pancho cackles along with the driver and exclaims, "Ella está loca!"

Spit glances at The Girl, who remains silent, face indifferent and emotionless. But then there's a glance, a moment of pleading eye contact that's unmistakable.

"Tell your friend she should be less crazy, yeah?" advises Pancho with a deadly serious look, "There are some real crazy people out here who are not to be messed with. Now where'd you want to go?"

"Anywhere that has a restroom," replies Spit, her bright smile barely hiding her wincing.

"You go along this way for just a minute, there's a diner just in a few miles, no problemo."

He shoots a charming look and looks her up and down.

She loses herself a little and tweaks back her hair, the atmosphere flirtatious.

"Gracias," she says, suggestively.

"Maybe we see you there, hey?" He suggests.

"Maybe."

"Tienes los ojos más bonitos del mundo," he says, romantically, "Me encantes."

"Eres tan cariñosa," she replies, flattered, "Muchas gracias."

She jogs back toward The Pickup as The Firebird pulls

away, and he leans out the window while looking back.

"Adiós bella!" He calls out with an amorous smile.

Spit climbs back inside The Pickup, looking rather pleased with herself.

The girls all look at her suggestively.

"What?" Asks Spit, turning defensive, "So he was a very nice man. Now drive, straight ahead, ándale!"

"Oh yeah," says Taylor, "you don't want her getting that seat wet, if you know what I mean."

A crummy wooden Diner so neglected it's barely standing with beat-up old cars dotted around the dirt car lot, a lonely half-dead cactus tree the most endearing feature.

The Pickup pulls in and skids to a halt.

The girls hop out and stretch while Spit hot-tails it to the entrance.

Inside, country music croons while customers sit lazily at tables that look like they haven't been cleaned since the place opened.

Spit bursts in and dashes into the restroom before Judge, Taylor and Memphis follow and cross to the counter where Bill, an old greaser in his 50's, cooks and smokes at the same time.

"Excuse me, sir," asks Judge, "where the hell are we right now?"

Bill points back out the door without even looking at her. "The sign out front and smell of off meat inside not a hint?" He replies. "This is Belle's Diner, honey."

She rolls her eyes and sighs, "I mean geographically."

He turns and looks at her dourly. "Oh, then why didn't you say?" he advises, "If you mean geographically, then you're in Belle's Diner, deep in the warm, sweaty butt crack of Southern California, just a groping uncle's finger slip from the puckered, greasy asshole that is Mexicali."

He nods toward the restroom. "No offense meant to your

friend, who just dashed by," he continues, "presumably either to evade our non-existent border patrol or to pull coke balloons out her hiney."

Judge shakes her head, shocked. "Wow, nice front of house you got there," she comments, "Say, would you be Belle by any chance? Because I don't see any other bitch working here."

Taylor and Memphis don't like the confrontation, but it's cool, Bill's actually impressed with Judge's moxie.

"I'm Bill," he explains, "I'm the boss, and you're in Bogie. You won't find it on a map because they only put the places people want to get to on maps. And you're standing in my diner, using my shitter, wasting my time."

Bill's got mouths to feed and stomachs to upset.

Judge ain't getting it, but Taylor takes the hint.

"We'll take four sodas," requests Taylor, "thanks."

Bill points to Taylor, impressed, and states, "She knows where she is."

Bill pops tops off bottles and plonks them on the counter with all the courtesy of a suicidal Hooter's waitress.

"What you doin'?" Judge asks Taylor, "We ain't staying."

Taylor swigs back on a soda and gasps, "Sorry, I couldn't help but get pulled in by the ambience. Besides, we ain't gonna make it now, no way."

Judge checks her watch and sighs.

Taylor peers at the nasty-looking meat cooking on the rusty hotplate. "Actually, thinking about it, Bill," she says, "that rotten beef smells good. You think you could burn the shit out of a piece and turn it into something resembling a burger?"

"Hell, it's the only thing I can do," replies Bill, "Something resembling a burger coming right up."

"Can I get one too?" Aks Memphis, "And can you like, hold the onions?"

"Honey, I can hold anything but the questionable

aftertaste."

Judge folds up the map and gives in as Bill tosses burgers.

"You want in on this, Soultrain?" He asks her.

Judge rolls her eyes and nods to confirm as such.

Spit exits the restroom to find Bill looking at her with a smirk.

He taps ash from his cigarette straight onto the floor. "Lookin' for something else to desperately fire out your ass, amigo?" He jokes.

Spit pauses and squints, confused.

One meal later, with The Girls all sitting around a table, Taylor finishes up.

"Well, based on that," she states, "there's a missing dog that ain't coming home."

She burps shamelessly before continuing, "Okay, splash and dash, people."

Taylor leaves for the restroom while Judge watches her.

Outside, unbeknownst to The Girls, who all have their backs to the window, a huge old Freightliner Tow Truck backs up to their Pickup before Thugs of various creeds get out and chain it up.

"Why's she suddenly in a hurry?" Questions Judge, the second Taylor is out of earshot, "Damn, she's testing my patience today."

"You should try riding in the back with her," suggests Spit.

"Don't be mean!" Argues Memphis, "She's just, being Taylor. I don't know."

Memphis casually turns and spots the Thugs outside. "Are you fucking kidding me!" She cries out.

She leaps up and runs out screaming. Judge and Spit run after her.

Taylor, having overheard the commotion, exits the restroom and joins the chase.

She bolts through the diner, bursts through the door, and sprints across the car lot on a mission as The Tow Truck drags The Pickup away backwards in a cloud of dust.

Memphis catches up with it as it slowly accelerates. "Hey, stop! Stop!" She yells.

She grabs The Pickup's front bumper and drags along with it.

Spit and Judge chase, but Judge can hardly run in her pencil skirt.

Spit trips over a pothole.

Taylor, sprinting like an Olympian, blows by them and climbs up onto The Pickup's hood.

"Don't scratch the paint!" Cries Memphis.

Fuck scratches. Taylor scrabbles up over the cab and drops into the bed.

As she gets back to her feet, Spit spots Hector, a bulky brute who looks like he could rape a grizzly bear, lean out the passenger window of the Tow Truck with a gun aimed at Memphis.

Spit pulls her pistol, aims quickly, and fires. BANG! BANG!

Hector flinches and fires back. BANG! BANG! BANG! A bullet skims the pickup's roof, carving a line in the paint.

"You'll pay for that!" Warns Memphis, still clinging to the bumper and dragging along pathetically.

Taylor leaps from the tailgate of the Pickup to the back of the Tow Truck and pauses to find green-blue dust all over her hands.

Judge, now way back from the chase, shuffles along like she's constipated.

Up on the Tow Truck, Taylor goes to make her way to the cab but freezes and stares.

The Firebird from before parked in the badlands ahead. Pancho sitting there watching.

He raises a rifle and takes aim for her.

Hector leans right out of his window and tries to get a scope on Memphis.

Spit fires again. BANG!

A shot pings by Hector, taking out the side mirror. He glares and ducks back inside.

Taylor's too exposed. She clambers back down the Tow Truck.

Pancho scopes her. She leaps for it. He fires and hits the pickup as she crashes back into the bed.

"For fuck's sake!" Screams Memphis, "Stop shooting my truck, you dick-fingered assholes!"

Taylor throws a few luggage cases out of the bed into the road. This is now just damage limitation.

BANG! A shot from Pancho's rifle glances by her and explodes the cab window. No time now. She's got to get off this ride.

She leaps the cab, slides down the windshield and hood, and grabs Memphis as she passes.

They both hit the ground and watch the Tow Truck growl away through the gears, the pickup dragging behind.

Memphis turns red with rage and screams, "I'll make a beanbag out of your ball sacks, you thieving fuck nuggets!"

Spit runs to them, and they stare, silent, defeated, and confused, as Judge finally catches up.

"Sorry," wheezes Judge, panting heavily, "can't run for shit in this, tight, ass, skirt."

"Well," summarises Taylor, "at least you probably left a great first impression."

The girls trudge back toward the Diner, pulling the luggage cases Taylor managed to salvage.

"Did you see that Firebird up ahead?" Aks Taylor, "It was those guys who gave Spit directions. They set us up."

"I saw you throwing your own damn cases out!" Replies Judge, "That's what I saw!"

* * *

The girls burst in, and Judge locks in on Bill.

He winces and sighs, "Ah shit."

"You want to explain to me what just happened, Bill?" Asks Judge, "You on parking permits round here or something? Because I sure as hell didn't see a damn ticket on our windshield."

"Right, before you start," he replies, "I'll bring your attention to the sign."

Bill presents a crudely made *NO-RESPONSIBILITY* sign.

"Now that thing cost me fifty bucks," he advises, "and it absolves me of any legal responsibility, okay?"

"The hell it does!" States Judge, "You bring it to court, bitch. You sit there with your stupid ass fifty-dollar sign while I explain the little racket you got going on here!"

"You think I'm behind this?" Exclaims Bill, "Seriously? You think I'd be choking people with burgers all day long if I was stealing fancy cars?"

"He's got a point," admits Taylor, "his food tastes like shit."

"Thank you!" Replies Bill before a pause, "…I think."

Judge folds her arms sternly and states, "Well, we're calling the cops, right now."

"Be my guest," applauds Bill, "in fact."

He snatches up a grubby old phone from behind the counter.

"Use my phone," he demands, "And good luck getting them to give a shit."

Judge grabs it from him. "Oh, I'll make them give a shit," she assures him.

"Why would the cops not care?" Asks Spit.

"Because they haven't cared the last dozen times," explains Bill, "These scumbags have been skulking round here for six months now, sniffing out what they can, takin' what they what." He turns a little dark and serious as he continues, "Taking who they want. It sure ain't conducive for repeat business, I can tell you that."

"Really?" Exclaims Spit, "Kidnapping?"

Bill raises his eyebrows. "Well, I'm not one to gossip," he replies, "but, there's an old latino lady on the outskirts of town, lives on the old farm. She's saying these guys took her daughter."

Spit remembers. The Girl in the back of the Firebird. That look in her eyes.

"I've seen her!" Declares Spit, "In the car, when I was getting directions. Wait, why don't the cops just arrest these assholes?"

Bill throws his hands up, defeated. "Nobody knows who they are," he rants, "They're as good as ghosts. Half of them are Mexican, so the police blame border patrol and border patrol blame the police. It's like a jerk circle at a uniform convention, and we're the ones getting fucked quietly in the basement."

"Aren't you guys worried they'll come in here?" Asks Taylor.

Bill confidently gazes around at his clientele and calls out, "Guys, are we worried those assholes will come in here?"

Clicking. Arming. Cocking. Every customer casually draws a weapon.

Judge slams down the phone and broods, "No answer."

Bill isn't surprised. He looks at Memphis concerned and asks, "You okay, Twilight?"

She clearly isn't. She's pale, pensive, and consumed.

"Seriously, I think I'm going to throw up," She groans.

"Hey, I did warn you about my burgers," he jokes, trying to make her smile.

She can't help but smirk.

He grabs a soda and candy bar and puts them on the counter. "Here you go," he says, "On the house."

"Thanks," she replies, somewhat touched, "that's really

sweet."

"Yeah, well, what can I say?" Sighs Bill, " Deep down, I'm the sappy emotional type."

He lights up a cigarette right there in his kitchen before he continues, "That's why I'm in hospitality."

The girls now out the back of the Diner by the dumpsters.

Judge lights a cigarette for Memphis, who takes a long, calming draw.

"I thought you quit?" Questions Spit.

"Yeah, well, you know what doctors don't tell you?" Replies Memphis, "Quitting smoking can seriously damage your mental health.

Taylor tries to brush away the green-blue dust on her top that was all over The Tow Truck.

"What the hell is this shit?" She complains.

A dog scampers around, causing Memphis to go from angry to delighted in an instant. It bounds up to her, and she strokes its head lovingly. "Was-your-name, hey?" She coos, "Was-your-name?"

She checks the collar and looks at the little copper tag, which reads 'Lily'.

"Hey, Lily!" Continues Memphis, "You're adorable, aren't you? Aren't you, yeah?"

She pauses and thinks, something clicking into place.

She then turns to Taylor and studies the dust on her top.

"What you thinking, Memphis?" Asks Judge.

Memphis reflects, "Back when I was a kid, my parents bought like, this old morgue. I mean, real old. Cool right? Anyway, I was helping clear it out, and there were hundreds of these little pots I had to move, full of ashes from the furnace, and they were covered in powder, seriously, just like that."

She clutches the dog's name tag as she continues, "And the pots, they were made of the same stuff as this, I swear."

"Jeeze, and I thought I had a messed up childhood," comments Taylor as she rolls her eyes.

"That's copper," explains Spit, "My dad's old ornaments are all made from it. It's a big thing back in Columbia."

"So, you saying these guys are held up in a morgue somewhere?" Winces Taylor, "Just how big are the bodies if they need a tow truck?"

Judge thinks for a moment and raises a finger. "No," she says, "but that could be the shit they dig out of the ground, right? Like from a a mine?"

The dog's owner walks out and calls over to the dog, "Lily? Hey, there you are!"

Judge fumbles out her map. "Excuse me, sir?" She asks the Dog Owner, "Do you happen to know of a Copper mine around here?"

"Copper mine?" He replies, amused, "Hell, you're in what used to be copper country, honey."

"Yeah?"

"Yeah! The big one though, round here, was Berro Bordo."

Judge taps the map, firmly. She's found it already. This is on.

The Dog Owner looks at them all, a little perplexed and asks, "What you girls want with a place like that anyhow? All you going to find up there is trouble and tumbleweeds."

"Well," says Memphis, "we sure aren't looking for tumbleweeds."

The Girls drag the battered travel cases Taylor managed to salvage into the neglected restroom.

"I ain't going dressed for the office," complains Judge, "hell no."

Taylor clicks open her case.

The others reel at a mess of dirty, crumpled-up clothes a tramp would sneer at.

"Woah!" Exclaims Memphis, "Oh my god Taylor!

Seriously, there are shoplifters who sort clothes more carefully than this."

"What's in the other case?" Asks Judge, pointing to an aluminum one.

Taylor defensively grabs it and clutches it tightly. "That's private," she responds, ominously.

The others are intrigued, but Taylor clearly doesn't want to talk about it.

"…Okaaaaaaaay then, Taylor," assures Judge, "We won't look in your dildo stash. I guess we now know why you were so motivated to save it in the first place."

Memphis unzips her case. Spit takes a pair of jeans out of it and holds them to her legs to find they're way too small.

"What the?" Gasps Spit, "Just how short are you, Memphis?"

"I'm five foot four and a half, okay?" Snaps Memphis, "Seriously, that's like average. You're the tall freaks."

Spit holds the jeans up and inspects them. "You mind if I modify these a little?" She asks.

"Fine, whatever," responds, Memphis.

Spit pulls out a flick knife and goes into a cubical.

Judge picks a few items and goes into the other.

Minutes later, Spit struts back out, wearing the jeans cut into shorts and a Gingham shirt knotted around her waist.

"So what do you think, ladies?" She asks with a twirl.

"Wow, Spit, you look amazing!" Assures Memphis, "You sure about the heels, though?"

"Shorts without heels?" Gasps Spit, appalled at the thought, "No bueno!"

The other door slowly creaks open, and Judge sheepishly walks out, wearing flared jeans with a bold cowboy belt buckle, a crop top, and a leather jacket. She looks just like Cleopatra Jones.

"Hey, Judge!" Sniggers Taylor, "Can you dig it?"

"These are your clothes, dumbass," responds Judge before looking in the mirror and smirking a little.

"How'd you plead," calls out Judge, "you jive sukas? Because the Judge is here to lay down the law!"

Bill flips burgers, and flicks sweat from his brow directly onto the hot plate.

He turns to find The Girls at the counter with a pleading look on their faces.

"Bill, we need to borrow a vehicle," says Taylor.

"What?.. Why?" He asks.

"Can we or can't we?" Demands Judge, "We got a lead on these assholes, okay, and we need to ask them a few questions."

"That right, SuperFly?" Questions Bill. "What you gonna ask them, trick or treat? How do I know can I trust you guys?"

They all pull out their dog-tags and show them to him.

He nods, impressed. "You all army?" He asks.

"Air army," confirms Judge.

He nods proudly and grabs his car keys. "Well, hoo-ah, ladies," he applauds, "You know what I like about the army? We're being terrorized, and you guys don't negotiate with terrorists."

He tosses the keys over to Judge. "White Caprice, try to bring the old piece of shit back in one piece."

The old wreck of a Caprice clatters along the empty highway with Memphis at the wheel.

Judge studies a map while Taylor and Spit in the back peer out the windows excited, pumped up for a fight.

"Is this where Judge somehow manages to accidentally direct us to our job interview?" Jokes Taylor.

Judge ignores that and points ahead. "Take this track coming up," she instructs.

The Caprice swerves off the highway and squirms up a gravel mountain track.

They pass a big red *DANGER OF DEATH* sign.

Judge tosses the map aside. "Bam!" She says with a smile. "Oh, we going to have a word with these tow truck fucks now."

Spit and Taylor take out their pistols and cock the slides.

"There it is!" Calls out Memphis, pointing out her Pickup parked up ahead on the crest.

The Caprice skids to a halt.

The girls stare ahead, fixed.

The huge looming Tow Truck pulls into the badlands near the Pickup, and Hector gets out with two filthy Skanks.

The Girls cautiously get out of the Caprice and stand in the wind, mean expressions on their faces and guns ready.

The buzzing of an engine gets everyone's attention.

The turn to see a Fat Thug, an obese, greasy, grotesque, man-pig, riding a tiny moped across the badlands ahead.

He takes up position with a rifle, his tongue hanging out. He's a real piece of shit.

"Now listen up!" Calls out Judge, "My name's Colonel Judith Newton of the US Air Force, and these girls are my crew! Now, you better hand back that vehicle, or we're going to be forced to call in a few favors from our good friend Uncle Sam, you dig?"

Hector glowers back in the distance and shouts back, "Fuck you!"

"That's your answer? That's the best you got, Triple A?"

"No, this is!"

The Skanks cross to the Pickup and open the doors.

"No!" Yells Memphis, "You stay the hell away, okay?"

The Skanks back away and slam the doors shut.

Flames flicker inside.

"You fucks!" Screams Memphis, "So help me god, I'll butcher you up like a blind organ thief, you whore's abortions!"

Hector points aggressively. "You come up here again," he warns, "the same happens to you!"

The Fat Thug spasms with mocking laughter. He rubs his big, wobbly, hairy belly, smearing sweat around it.

Memphis fucking loses it. "You stupid, skanky ass bitches!" She shouts as she goes Charles Bronson and pulls her Glock.

This just became open season on Skanks.

She opens fire. BANG! BANG! BANG! BANG! BANG! BANG!

The Skanks flee to the Tow Truck.

BANG! Hector fires back.

BANG! BANG! The Fat Thug fires.

Judge, Spit, and Taylor run behind The Caprice and cover Memphis as shots ping around her.

Spit scopes The Fat Thug reloading. BANG! She fires at him.

The round misses. He cackles and buzzes away on his moped.

"The hell with this!" Shouts Taylor, having had enough.

She crosses to the trunk, pulls out that mysterious aluminum case, crouches down, and swings it open.

"Oh, no, you didn't!" Exclaims Judge.

Taylor pops back up with a battered old Vietnam-era rocket launcher on her shoulder.

"Ay caramba!" Yells Spit.

"Memphis! Get the fuck out the way!" Shouts Taylor.

Memphis turns, sees the rocket launcher, and hits the deck.

Hector can't believe it. He freezes.

Taylor aims for him and fires.

WOOOOOOOSH! A rocket shrieks from the launcher.

The Fat Thug on the scooter rides straight into the rocket's path.

BOOOOOOOM! He pops like an over-packed sack of giblets.

The girls stare, stunned, as meat slops down to the ground.

Hector snaps from his freeze, runs to the Tow Truck, and climbs in.

He's outta there. The Tow Truck fires up and roars away, leaving the place in a solemn silence.

The girls slowly walk around The Caprice and drink in the eerie scene before them.

A twenty-foot circle of scattered blood and guts surrounds the charred smoking moped.

CRASH! Fat Thug's rifle clatters back down to Earth.

"Well," says Spit, "that intensity intensified."

Memphis gazes hopelessly at the burning Pickup.

"You okay, Memphis?" Asks Spit.

Memphis turns to Taylor in a fit of rage. "Why?" She yells, "Why couldn't you do that before they burnt my truck, you retarded fucking redneck?"

Taylor winces. Memphis has a point.

Judge stands fixed, still processing the bloody scene. "Am I high?" she wonders out loud, "Or did you really just frag a fat Mexican with an RPG?"

"You should be thanking me!" Argues Taylor, "That was clearly self-defense!"

"Self-defense?" Questions Judge, "So, that's what you'd call reasonable force?"

"Where the hell did you get that thing?" Asks Spit, staring at the rocket launcher as smoke still wafts from it.

"At a yard sale," reveals Taylor.

"What kind of yard sale sells rocket launchers?" Asks Spit.

"The kind you find in Texas," replies Taylor, "And it's not even mine, I'm transporting it for friend."

Judge massages her temples, growing increasingly stressed.

"Oh! That's great, Taylor!" She cries out, "That's real great! So we can add arms dealing to the charge of murder now, can we?"

Memphis paces back and forth, fuming.

Spit gazes at the Pickup as the licking flames gradually die out.

Hey," she says to Memphis, pointing it out, "it's not so bad, look."

Memphis looks back at her Pickup with hope in her eyes, just as the fuel tank erupts into a roaring fireball.

Spit cringes.

"Well, that's it," concludes Judge, throwing her hands up, defeated and pacing around, "we're all going to prison! I hope you're happy, Taylor. Mind you, prison's probably summer camp to you! Not for me. Oh, I got plenty of enemies locked up there waiting for my black ass!" She points to Memphis and continues. "She's probably going to be put in a mental ward! Spit, I sure hope you like eighteen-stone butch lesbians and badly carved strap-ons! Welcome to the rest of your lives, ladies!"

They all stare silently as birds swoop down to eat the scattered flesh.

"Guys, this asshole, he was a criminal, right?" Reasons Spit, "And the police, they don't care what's happening out here. So, who gives a fuck?"

They all stare at Spit, shocked. Did she just say that?

Taylor crosses over, proudly puts an arm around her, and states, "See? See! Even the Mexicans-"

"-Columbians-" interjects Spit.

"-COLUMBIANS are on our side here," continues Taylor, "All we've done is defend ourselves. Defend ourselves as vulnerable women in a hostile environment."

Judge rolls her eyes.

Taylor presents a nearby crow tucking into over-cooked pieces of Mexican. "And look, the wildlife is even cleaning up the evidence for us!" she argues, "We're not criminals, we're the good guys. If anything, we're conservationists. That thing's probably close to extinction, Judge. That's the best meal it's ever had. Look at him, pecking away there. I can see him growing stronger by the second, and-"

"Just shut the hell up, okay?" Barks Judge, "Point taken, you've made your case. Let's just get out of here."

They all wander back to the Caprice.

"But what about my truck?" Asks Memphis, "Can't they like, trace it back to me? We can't leave it here like this."

Taylor, Judge, and Spit exchange a few nods.

Taylor sighs and takes a rocket from the case.

"No!" Pleads Memphis, "I meant take it with us! Please, Taylor, no!"

Taylor walks toward the Pickup, crouches, aims, and fires.

WOOSH! BOOM! The Pickup explodes. Fragments fire everywhere.

Taylor closes her eyes as debris clatters down around her.

Memphis stands frozen and seething as Taylor walks back over and offers her the charred Pink Power Ranger figure.

"You've got insurance, right?" Asks Taylor.

Memphis snatches the figure, speechless with contempt.

They go to get back in the Caprice, but Judge pauses and narrows her eyes as she looks back to the crest of the mountain.

"Hold up a second," she says, "let's just see what they're hiding over there."

Chapter 3

The girls walk to the crest and stare down at a tiny, abandoned mine town where wooden shacks swarm with dozens of Thugs going about their ominous business.

The Tow Truck pulls up in a cloud of dust, and Hector leaps out, animated and angry, as Pancho exits one of the buildings to deal with him.

"Oh, hello. It's our old friend," says Taylor.

Pancho bosses everyone around and points back up at The Girls.

Memphis glares back and gives him both middle fingers.

Spit sighs, "Why is it always the handsome ones?"

Pancho grabs The Young Mexican Girl from one of the Thugs. She fights back.

"Look! That's her!" Exclaims Spit, pointing her out, "That's the girl I saw! Does she look like she wants to be here, eh, eh?"

Pancho shoves The Girl through the door of an old bar.

"Well, here goes the neighborhood," concludes Taylor as she grabs the rocket launcher.

"Woah!" Yells Judge, "Cool it now, Rambo! We've had more than enough rocket launcher action for one day."

Taylor shakes her head. "Judge, you've got no authority out here," she argues, "and these dicks have got my trigger finger itching."

"Yeah, well, finger your own trigger for a few minutes," orders Judge. "Hell, we don't what we're messing with here. For all we know, they could have hostages hidden everywhere."

Judge slowly stares Taylor down.

"Let's return to base," advises Judge, "get ourselves a clue, get ourselves a plan, and if this looks like what it is, girl, we're gonna scratch that itch of yours, okay?"

Taylor can get on board with that.

Spit leans into Memphis, cups her mouth, and remarks, "Did she just call the diner "base"?"

"Seriously, you've tasted the food, right?" Responds Memphis, "You think it's fairer to call that place a diner?"

Inside the near derelict old bar, with music serenading from a crackling jukebox, Pancho casually pours a shot with The Girl by his side and his arm around her.

He looks up at Hector and the Skanks, who stand shamefaced in front of him.

"You let four women just walk in here and kill that fat retard?" he hisses, "What are you, little pussies?"

They remain silent as he continues, "You owe me a truck. You can move a lot of shit in a beast like that."

Hector shakes his head and stutters, "How were we supposed to-"

"-Fuck your excuses, yeah?" Barks Pancho, "Now I got to make calls. You make me work too hard fixing up your shit."

He glares up at the Skanks, who stare back indifferently.

"What you think you staring at," he sneers, "you pig ugly bitches?"

He necks his shot and forces himself upon The Girl, his lips slurping all over hers. It's pretty gross.

The Skanks roll their eyes.

* * *

All back in the Caprice and headed to The Diner, The Girls sit somberly in silence.

Judge suddenly spots something ahead. It's a farm, outside of which Mrs Martinez, an old Mexican lady, is painting a fence.

"Hey, pull over," demands Judge, "I want to have a word with Old El Paso here."

The Caprice pulls up at the farm's entrance, and The Girls get out.

Mrs Martinez looks back warily, clearly afraid of strangers.

"Ma'am, can I ask you a few questions?" Asks Judge.

"Sí," Replies Mrs Martinez, still very cautious.

"We're looking for a lady who says her daughter's been kidnapped, is that, by any chance, you?"

Mrs Martinez's eyes widen, and she nods, surprised.

"You got a picture we can see?" Asks Judge.

Mrs Martinez fumbles through her pocket, pulls out a tattered picture, and hands it across.

They all study it. It's The Girl alright.

"I work here for many years for Mr Everdeen," explains Mrs Martinez, "Very kind. But he get sick and he pass away. Everything he leaved to me. He a rich man. So I give all the monies to these men who come round here. They say they bring my daughter from Mexico to me. But as soon as we are together, they take her again, and police, no interested in my problem. She maybe not even alive."

"She's alive, anciana!" Announces Spit, "We seen her."

Mrs Martinez drops her paintbrush and covers her mouth. "Dios mío!" She gasps.

Judge looks at her frankly and explains, "She's in some trouble, okay? But we're army, and it's trouble we're lookin' to do something about."

"Army?" Exclaims Mrs Martinez, "Oh, gracias! Muchas gracias!"

Judge leans to Taylor and says, "Well, looks like you got your wish."

"Oh, come on," scoffs Taylor, "admit it, you're loving this even more than me."

Memphis raises her hand. "I'm not ashamed to say I'm on board, if only for the payback," she admits.

"So, are we going for it?" Asks Spit, "We gonna save this girl? Really?"

The girls all nod and try to hide their delight that some action has come their way.

Judge turns to Mrs Martinez and thumbs down the road. "Look, if you need us, we're hanging out at Belle's diner. You know it?" She asks.

Mrs Martinez thinks and gestures, gagging on her finger.

"Yeah," concludes Memphis, "she knows it."

The Caprice skids to a halt outside The Diner.

As the girls enter, Judge takes Taylor to one side so she can speak to her alone.

"Okay," informs Judge, "you got some explaining to do, girl. A rocket launcher? What's all that about?"

Taylor looks side to side to make sure no one's listening in and explains, "Look, I'm a prepper, okay? You know what that is?"

"Really? Like on the pornos, where they, you know?"

Judge crudely mimes a blow-job.

"No!" Exclaims Taylor, "not a fluffer! I'm part of this secret prepper group. Something real big is going to happen soon, economic collapse, natural disaster, war, but most probably zombies. We've got foxholes around the state. So when the shit hits the fan, we're leaving town and digging in."

"That's some paranoid bullshit, you know that?"

"Whatever, I was going to drop it off at one of these locations, but then you had to take us off on the runaround, didn't you?"

Judge thinks for a moment. "And this foxhole, there'd be some firepower hidden there?" She asks.

"Look, all I've got is some co-ordinates, some notes, and a few people's word," explains Taylor, "There could be nothing there but sharp sticks and rape alarms for all I know."

"Okay, well, we'll find out where it is, and we'll check it out."

Judge crosses to the center of the diner.

"Can I get ya'll attention, please?" She requests.

The Customers all pause and look up.

"Your little gang problem you got here," she continues, "well, it turns out it's a lot bigger than you think, but the good news is, we're here to fix it."

"Just who the hell are you girls?" Asks a confused diner.

The girls stand proudly together as Judge proudly declares, "Sir, we're Hell's Belles."

The Customers erupt into roaring laughter.

"Yeah, you laugh it up all you like," sneers Judge, "We've sent those guys a clear message. Now, thankfully, the police don't want to get involved, so all we're asking is you help us make sure it stays that way."

She nods smugly as a Cop Car pulls up outside the window behind her.

A Sheriff gets out, takes off his shades, and scans around suspiciously before entering.

Everyone stays silent as the door creaks shut, and his boots clump along the wooden floorboards before easing to a halt.

"The station received a missed call from here?" informs The Sheriff, "There a problem?"

Bill goes wide-eyed and looks to Judge.

"Oh yeah, there's a problem," responds Judge, trying to come up with a cover story, "We…umm."

She points to Bill and blurts out, "We want to press

charges against this asshole for poor hygiene."

Bill's cigarette droops in his mouth.

"Poor hygiene?" Questions the Sheriff.

"Uh-huh!" Confirms Judge, thinking on her feet, "We witnessed him go to the restroom, and we did not hear him wash his hands... and he was in there a real long time. We think he was, you know, rubbing the unicorn's horn."

The Sheriff looks back, confused.

Judge winces and looks to the girls for backup.

"Riding the great white knuckler," says Taylor.

"Engaging in hand-to-gland combat," says Spit.

"Causing a dishonorable discharge," says Memphis.

"Officer," continues Judge, trying to appear serious and offended, "we believe he was holding his sausage hostage."

Bill chokes.

The Sheriff winces and rubs the back of his neck. "Well, that's not really our department," he explains, "Anyhow, we've had a few calls in today. We'll be keeping a close eye around here. Just thought I'd let you all know that."

He locks eyes with Judge for a moment and leaves.

The second the door shuts, diners go back to chatting and eating while The Girls cross over to Bill.

Bill stares at them, forlornly and sighs, "You want to tell me why, after six months trying to get that man through this door, when he finally shows up, we give him a reason to put me on a sex-offenders register?"

"Look," explains Judge, "we spoke to your local towing company, and the situation well... It kinda blew up."

He scans across their frank looks and rolls his eyes.

"And ask yourself this," she continues, "the cops show no interest for all this time, then we start poking a few bushes, and suddenly they're showing up over a missed call? Don't that seem a little odd to you?"

"You think the cops are in on this?" Asks Spit

Judge shoots them all a serious look and replies, "All I'm

saying is this whole thing smells fishier than Taylor's luggage case."

"I'm right here, you know?" Complains Taylor.

"Yeah," acknowledges Judge, "so how about you get us some drinks while we work out where this foxhole of yours is?"

Taylor leans on the counter as the others cross over to a table.

"Your foxhole?" Asks Bill with a suggestive grin.

"Yeah," confirms Taylor, "you suddenly need to go visit the restroom?"

Minutes later, Taylor crosses back to the table with a tray of drinks.

"You know what I've just realized?" She announces as she sets the tray down, "We're the actual freakin' real-life A-Team."

They fall silent and exchange glances, before all saying at the same time, "I'm Face!!"

"No, I'm Face!" They all shout again.

"Actually, I already got this worked out," reveals Taylor, "I'm the best looking, so I have to be Face."

"Erm, no," argues Memphis, "Spit is the prettiest."

Spit and Memphis exchange warm smiles.

Taylor shakes her head dismissively, "No, Spit can only be one person," she argues, "because there was only ever one Mexican in the A-Team."

"Columbian, she's Columbian," sighs Judge, "Why can't you grasp this concept?"

"I'm Daisy Duke," claims Spit, "she was Hispanic."

"Right, okay," explains Taylor, "you can't be Daisy Duke for two reasons, Spit. One, she was from Georgia, and two, she wasn't actually in the A-Team."

"The actress was part Latino," argues Spit, "That's why she was so beautiful."

Taylor sighs, "Can someone explain the rules to Spit, please."

"Rules?" Questions Judge, "Do you not think we have more pressing issues right now?"

"That would be cool, though," wonders Memphis, "Dukes Of Hazard in the A-Team, right?"

Taylor dismisses the comment, turns to Spit, and says, "Look, at best, you can be persecuted farm worker."

Judge folds her arms, "Okay, genius," she challenges, "if you think you're Face, who the hell am I?"

Taylor looks at Judge deadpan. "Seriously?" She asks.

"Oh, did we just go there?" Exclaims Judge, "Are we doing this? It comes down to that, you simple-ass redneck fool!"

Taylor points to everyone, "Fool, she said fool. You all heard that, right?"

Judge stares incredulously at Taylor, "You're the one all up in people's faces, kicking their ass." She argues, "Hell, you're big old Taylor T. You actually are Miss T."

Taylor sneers.

Memphis shakes her head and sighs, "Don't make me Murdock, Taylor. I'm not being Murdock, okay?"

"How can you not be Murdock?" Questions Taylor, "You're a pilot, and you're crazy."

Memphis bounces in her seat, fists clenched, "Quit saying that!" She moans, "I'm highly introverted, and yes, that's a thing! Why don't you look it up, you idiot?"

"Oh yeah, clearly!" Mocks Taylor, "That was a real introverted response."

"Screw you, Taylor!" Barks Memphis, "Seriously, it's about how you process things."

Taylor looks Memphis right in the eye and says, "Well, process this, you're cat-shit-crazy, end of conversation."

Memphis shakes her head, frustrated. She can't win.

Judge points at Taylor accusingly and states, "Murdock

was a redneck, you're a redneck, you're Murdock."

"Yeah?" Responds Taylor, "Enjoying your MILKshake there Judge? Thinking about how you ain't gonna get on no plane."

Judge shakes her head, deplored. "You're unbelievable, you know that? Unbelievable." She says, "Look, we got to move out, okay? So come on, enough of this bullshit, let's go."

They sigh, defeated, neck their drinks, and go to leave.

"Who are we kidding?" Concludes Memphis, "We're all Murdock, aren't we?"

They let that one hang and leave.

The Caprice parked deep within in the badlands where no buildings can be seen and no trace of human life exists.

Taylor leads the girls into the desert, following her notes to an innocent-looking rock.

The girls move it away to find a hidden piece of rope.

"So, what's supposed to be here?" Asks Judge.

Taylor checks her notes again and reads, "A couple of m-fifteens and whatever the fuck an m-one-nine-seven is."

Memphis and Spit pull away a panel.

They all stare down into a hole underneath it.

"Well, that'll be whatever the fuck an m-one-nine-seven is," exclaims Judge.

Six-foot of forty-year-old Gatling gun stares back at them.

Judge shakes her head and states, "Okay, that ain't prepping, that's a goddamn uprising."

Memphis and Spit retrieve old dusty assault rifles.

"Hey, look," says Memphis, "some radios too."

Judge nods, impressed. "Okay, not bad," she admits, "cover it back up."

"What? We're leaving this?" Questions Taylor, gesturing to the massive Gatling gun.

"You a Terminator now?" Asks Judge, "You going to run

around with that thing? You're a liability as it is."

Spit thumbs back to the Caprice. "How would we even fit that in the car, eh?" She points out.

"Fine," sighs Taylor, "I can never have fun things."

Taylor stares down, disappointed, as Memphis and Spit slide the panel back over the crate.

As The Caprice approaches the Diner, a siren sounds, and a Cop Car scrabbles out from bushes to take chase.

The Girls all glance around, surprised.

"You want me to pull over?" Asks Memphis, "'Cause we've got a trunk full of rifles, and I'm all out of dick jokes."

"Hell yeah," replies Judge, "Let's see what he wants."

The Caprice eases to a halt, and The Cop Car pulls up behind.

Out steps The Sheriff who moseys slowly up to the window.

Judge smiles back. "There something we can help you with, officer?" She asks.

"This your vehicle?" He questions.

"We're borrowing it, from Bill. Why you wanna know?"

"Could you all step out, please?"

The Girls all look nervously to Judge.

"Why?" She asks.

He looks the Caprice up and down and replies, "I need to perform a search of this vehicle."

"The hell you do?" argues Judge, "On what grounds?"

He stares blankly back.

"You got a warrant?" She asks.

"I'm just trying to serve my community, ma'am," he states.

"Oh, I'm sure you are," replies Judge, "but you overstep your jurisdiction with us again, and I'll make sure you'll be serving your community... over a fast food counter. You dig?"

She stares him down. Lawyered.

Finally, back at The Diner, The Girls walk in, and Bill snaps straight around from his hotplate with a note.

"Excellent, Charlie and his angels," he announces, "you got a message. Old lady Martinez, she wants you guys to meet her on the farm. Sounded pretty urgent."

The girls look at each other. Off they go again.

"Thanks, Bill," replies Judge as she heads back out the door, "Hey, cancel my five-o-clock will ya, sugar tits?"

"Oh, sure thing," quips Bill, "You still good for your prostate exam in the morning?"

He watches Judge leave and smiles to himself.

With the evening now drawing in and basking the empty paddock of the disused farm in a beautiful reddish light, The Girls roll up in the Caprice as Mrs Martinez gets out an old GMC van and greets them.

She leads them to a barn and unlocks a padlock.

"I remember after you go," explains Mrs Martinez, "Mr Everdeen, he put this away long time ago when he first got ill. He love this thing so much before, but you say you air army, so maybe…"

The huge wooden door swings open, and The Girl's jaws drop.

"I sure wasn't expecting that," says Spit.

They all stare at a dusty old Huey helicopter that's been stored away for years.

"Old-skool!" Applauds Taylor, "Freaking A!"

"Is good to you, yeah?" Asks Mrs Martinez.

Judge slowly nods and smiles. "Oh, you done good, Mrs Martinez," she states, "You done real good."

Memphis looks unimpressed, so Judge takes her to one side.

"I know it ain't Big Greasy," says Judge, "but you can dig on this, right?"

Memphis gestures at the civilian spec Huey. "It's got no weapons," she complains, "Seriously, what are we going to do with it? Dust these guy's crops?"

Judge smiles coyly, "Got no weapons YET," she replies with a smirk.

She nods to the van and calls back to the others, "Now, does anybody know where I might find whatever the fuck an m-one-nine-seven is?"

With crickets chirping in the moonlit badlands, the old GMC Van backs up and skids to a halt.

The girls leap out, pull the panel off the hidden crate, and quickly heave the Gatling gun out into the van.

The Van screeches back onto the road and roars into the night.

Memphis pensively drives, Judge beside her, Taylor and Spit sitting with the Gatling gun in the back.

"Okay," advises Judge, "let's stay under the limit. We don't want to attract the attention of-"

WHOOP! WHOOP! Blue and red lights flash behind.

Memphis glares into her side mirror. "Seriously, who just so happens to be patrolling the middle of nowhere at this time?" She wonders.

They all look at each other, suspiciously.

"Okay, poker faces, ladies," orders Judge.

The Van eases to a halt, and the Cop Car pulls up behind.

Out steps The Sheriff, who strolls up to the Van.

"You girls, running an overnight delivery service?" Asks The Sheriff.

"You interested?" Replies Judge, "Is there a warrant you hoping to have to sign for?"

"Oh, I ain't looking for no warrant. You think I need a warrant to search this here vehicle, miss?"

"I know you need a warrant, asshole."

"You'd think that now, wouldn't you? But then you see, Patriot Act allows me to investigate anything I deem highly suspicious behavior."

"The Patriot Act! Do we look like terrorists to you?"

He tries to lean in the window to take a closer look, but Memphis blocks him, tweaks her hair back, and smiles awkwardly.

Judge points at The Sheriff. "Now I suggest," she advises, "unless you actually witness us doing something that, without a doubt, requires your intervention, you back the hell off, okay?"

He locks eyes with Judge. She knows she's got him but-

CHACHACHACHACHACHACHACHACHA! The Gatling gun discharges rounds straight through the metal rear doors of the Van.

He snaps around to find a light on the Cop Car shot out.

"Bye!" Exclaims Memphis as she floors the accelerator.

The Van screeches away while he runs to his Cop Car.

Judge glares back at Taylor and Spit as the tired old engine clatters.

"Just what the hell was that?" She asks.

Spit looks back innocently and replies, "I was just holding it when it went off in my hands!"

"Come to think of it," ponders Taylor, "the guy who told me about this, did warn me it was a little flaky."

Judge shakes her head at Taylor and peers into her mirror.

"Well, is he following?" Asks Judge.

"No," scoffs Taylor, "he's gone to write us a ticket and send it in the mail, Judge. What do you think?"

Memphis watches her mirror and winces. "Here he comes!" she warns.

Blue and red lights fill the back windows and-

BANG! The Cop Car rams the Van hard, throwing The Girls forward.

"Damn it!" Shouts Judge, "Floor it!"

Memphis looks back at her, frustrated and yells, "What do you think I'm doing here?"

"Just lose him!" Orders Judge, "And no crazy shit!"

Memphis thinks for a moment and cuts the wheel hard.

The Van races down the dirt track. The Cop Car follows.

The Sheriff pulls out a Mach-10, aims out his window, and fires.

BWATATATATATATATATATAT! Bullets ping off the Van as Memphis fights with the wheel.

Judge ducks in her seat. "You want to tell me what kind of cops carry full-auto machine guns?" She exclaims.

The Van ramps a mound of dirt and lands hard.

CHACHACHACHA! The Gatling gun fires.

The Cop Car swerves the mound as bullets punch into the dirt.

Memphis suddenly has an idea. She peers ahead and guns it.

"HOLD ONTO YOUR TITS!" She shouts.

"Memphis," warns Judge, "I said no crazy shit!"

Their eyes bulge. The Van ramps another huge mound and sails majestically through the air with dirt trailing from it.

The Cop Car swerves the mound.

The Van lands. CHACHACHACHACHACHACHA!

Bullets spark off the Cop Car as The Sheriff fires back.

The girls all hold on tight and wince as Memphis grits her teeth and aims for another even bigger mound.

The Van leaps, flies through the star-filled, dark blue sky for a few long moments, everyone going weightless inside, and crashes down hard, bottoming out the suspension. CHACHACHACHACHACHACHA!

The Cop Car takes multiple hits. It loses a tire, swerves, catches the dirt, and kicks up into a spectacular roll, spinning over and over as body panels tear away, and eventually comes to rest in a twisted heap.

Spit and Taylor watch the cloud of dust disappear in the distance.

"I've never been so happy over a premature discharge!" Announces Spit.

The Van skids back onto an asphalt road and slews sideways.

The Gatling Gun slides around inside and hits one side of the load space. CHACHACHACHACHACHA!

Taylor and Spit cower out of its way.

Rounds chop holes into the bodywork and-

WOOOOOOOOMPH!

The Van clatters down the road with the rear quarter on fire

Taylor and Spit desperately kick at flames.

"Can I get off at the next stop, please?" Shouts Taylor.

Memphis grips the wheel with determination and shouts, "Wait! We're nearly there!"

The Van slews into the farm, burning like a torch.

Memphis peers ahead and smiles. "Perfect!" She says to herself.

A peaceful pond in the moonlight under a picturesque little tree. A small wooden rowing boat to one side. Insects chirp.

The Van crashes through a fence, hits the boat, misses the pond, and rolls over in a cloud of dust.

The girls cough in a heap in the van, the fire now smothered out.

"Real slick, Memphis," Groans Taylor, "You know, the fire service are always lookin' for volunteers."

Memphis hangs proudly from her seat buckle and says. "Well, you know what they say: stop, drop and roll, right?"

The Gatling Gun jolts. They all wince. Nothing.

"Okay, well," summarises Judge, "bar the firefight with the police, writing off Mrs Martinez's van and some minor boat-related damage; I'm classing this mission as a technical success. Nice work, ladies."

While an animal howls at the midnight moon, the lights flick off inside The Diner, chairs stacked on tables, everything put away for the night, and The girls on the floor, shuffling into sleeping bags.

"You'll have to forgive the lack of cookies and Hannah Montana DVD's," apologises Bill, "I've never hosted a sleepover before."

Judge gets herself comfortable and smiles thankfully at him. "Thanks for putting us up, Bill," she says.

"Like I said," he continues, "my trailers far more accommodating. You girls any good at Twister?"

"And like I said, we're not safe to be around right now," replies Judge.

"Thanks, Bill," calls out Spit.

"Night, Bill," echoes Taylor.

"Sleep tight," adds Memphis.

Bill goes to leave, looks back disappointed, and sighs, "Guess I'm just going to have to miss the naked pillow fight then."

The Sheriff lies on his back out the shattered window of the wrecked Cop Car, a real bloody mess, choking for this life, one of the emergency lights on the roof still pulsing.

"Fuckin' pigs, man!" Rants Pancho, who's now arrived with a crew of Thugs, "They useless as shit in this country!"

He snatches the Mach 10 from the ground.

BANG! He shoots The Sheriff in the head.

Hector carefully inspects the wreckage. "You seen the size of the entry holes on this thing?" He asks, looking somewhat worried.

The Sheriff whimpers a little.

BANG! Pancho puts him down for good.

"Jeeze," Exclaims Pancho," he can't even die right, you know? Fucking amateur."

"I got some reservations here," worries Hector.

Pancho sighs and rolls his eyes. "They are just fuckin' women," he replies, "Stop being such a little puto, yeah?"

They cross to the Firebird and Tow Truck, where a whole crew are waiting with guns.

Inside The Diner, a tap drips and a bug zapper occasionally buzzes.

Spit lies wide awake in her sleeping bag, with Memphis snoring loudly next to her.

She turns over to find Judge staring back.

"How can someone so tiny make so much noise?" Whispers Spit.

"At least she's finally stopped farting," Judge replies, "I lost my damn earplugs with my case."

They both let out a long mutual sigh and stare at the ceiling, unable to sleep.

The sound of engines roaring in the distance gradually grows louder.

"You hear that?" Asks Spit, her eyes widening.

Headlights illuminate the windows. Tires skid. Voices outside.

"Heads up!" Yells Judge.

Taylor bolts upright, the M15 she's been sleeping with ready in her hands.

She stares at Memphis, gazing back sleepily, who's then slid away as Judge and Spit drag her behind the counter.

RATATATATATATATATATAT! Rounds fire through the walls.

Taylor slips out her bag and dives over the counter.

Bullets tear through The Diner, exploding windows, bottles, and jars.

The girls cower as glass and debris showers over them.

Then silence.

"Estoy hasta la madre!" Calls out Pancho, "You hear that? I had enough of, you stupid shit stinking bitches!"

Taylor takes up position on the counter with her gun ready to unleash hell, but Judge pulls her back down.

"If any of you are still alive, you listen, yeah?" Continues Pancho, "You don't mess with us, okay? You don't know what you messing with! So run home to your madres and padres where you belong."

Footsteps. Doors slam. Vehicles leave.

Taylor runs to the door and peers through a small gap.

The Firebird and Tow Truck's tail lights fade away into the darkness.

Memphis lets out a huge yawn and stretches.

"So much for a decent night's sleep," she sighs, "am I right?"

Spit and Judge glare back at her.

With the sun rising, Bill's Caprice pulls up outside The Diner.

He gets out warily and takes in the scene of his bullet-riddled eatery before cautiously walking up to the door and peering in.

The girls stare back from behind the counter, guns aimed.

He scans around the destruction, horrified as they realise it's him and drop their weapons.

"And here's me showing up early to make you all breakfast," he groans.

The girls crunch over the glass and comfort him.

"Seriously, we're so sorry," says Memphis.

"We'll help you clean it up, okay?" Assures Spit.

He lets out a long sigh and remarks, "Well, this puts my whole Michelin star dream back another year."

* * *

Now back in the Barn at the Farm, The girls struggle to mount the Gatling Gun to the Huey.

Spit heaves it up while Taylor tries to fasten a bolt.

Spit slips and catches her hand. "Jeeze! Taylor, you idiot!" She barks.

They drop the gun to the ground, and Taylor slams down her wrench.

"If I had the right size wrench, this would be easy," complains Taylor, "I said I need a one-and-one-fifth, Memphis."

"And, like I already explained to you three times!" Shouts Memphis, "There's no such thing as a fuckin' one-and-one-fifth wrench, Taylor! Okay?"

Taylor throws up her arms and takes in the scene. "Well, a fine fucking montage this has turned out to be," she groans, "Just what are we doin' here? I mean, they came back real strong last night, who knows just what we're messing with."

Judge folds her arms and shakes her head at Taylor. "Girl, this whole thing started because your stupid ass popped a fat Mexican on a scooter, okay?" She reminds her, "Don't forget that."

"Oh, I'm to blame?" Questions Taylor, "Who got us here in the first place, Judge? Who got us lost? You! And why? Because you're a control freak!"

"She's right, Judge," confirms Memphis, "you like, always have to be the boss of everybody."

Judge angrily points at Memphis. "You! You need to shut your mouth!" she warns, "It's the crazy shit you're always pulling that got us disenrolled in the first place!"

Memphis stamps her feet and cries, "Seriously, stop calling me crazy!"

"You are fuckin' crazy," states Taylor, "you crazy little crazy bitch!"

Memphis glares up at Taylor, teeth gritted, and hisses, "Taylor, I don't care how much bigger than me you are, I will scratch your fucking eyes out!"

"Good luck trying to reach," scoffs Taylor, "you pint-size problem child."

"You bitch!" Screams Memphis, "You fuckin' bitch! I'm five foot four and a half!"

Memphis starts crying.

Judge rolls her eyes. "And out comes the Valley brat," she sighs.

"I thought we stuck up for each other?" Whimpers Memphis, "I thought we were friends?"

Spit puts her arms around Memphis to comfort her and glares at the other two.

"Back off her, okay?" Demands Spit, "She's right, this is nobody's fault!"

"You think?" Questions Judge, "You want to know why this whole problem existed in the first place? Because somebody thought you needed protecting from us, because apparently we're a bad influence!"

Spit gestures at the guns and helicopter. "Well, maybe they're right, yeah?" she argues, "I mean, look at this shit. I spend one day out of the force with you guys, and now I'm strapping a Gatling gun to a helicopter?"

"She's right, Judge," agrees Taylor, "You've lost control of this whole situation!"

"I'm fixing this whole situation!" Exclaims Judge, "I'm trying to keep your ass out of jail, you idiot! And you know what? Let's turn ourselves in, let's go to trial! And you know what, you can represent yourself!"

Taylor shrugs, nonchalantly. "Fine with me!" she says, "Three letters, PMT, every woman's get out of jail free card!"

"Damn, you're an idiot!" Sighs Judge.

"Yeah," adds Spit, "and you'd actually have to prove you have a chocha anyway."

Taylor gets right in Spit's face. "Well, it's a shame I'm not you then, isn't it?" She states, "Because then they could just ask pretty much anybody in the force as an eye witness."

Memphis wriggles out of Spit's arms and squares up to Taylor ."Seriously, Taylor!" She barks, "That's crossing a line!"

Spit starts to take her hooped earrings out, ready to fight. "Fuck you, you redneck fuckin' hijuepuerca!" She cusses, "You want to go? You think I'm scared of you, 'Taylor Trash'?"

Taylor stares back ominously, eyes intense, "What did you just call me?" She asks in a threatening tone.

Taylor and Spit circle one another and launch into a furious catfight, complete with schoolgirl hair pulling until Memphis and Judge manage to drag them apart.

"Enough! Enough!" Demands Judge, standing between them all. "Now, I appreciate everyone's a little tired, but damn, you girls, got to get with the program!"

They all look to the floor as Judge stares at them, sincerely. "You know what?" she says, "Taylor, you are too aggressive. Spit, when you're around guys, you do lose focus. And, Memphis, I ain't calling you crazy, girl, but sometimes, you actually pull some crazy shit. And you know what, I'm a bossy black bitch, okay? But that ain't such a bad thing."

The girls stare back, panting.

"Is this a dumb fucked up situation we've got ourselves in?" continues Judge, "Hell yeah. But you know what? Dumb fucked up situations are our bread and butter. And if it's fighting for our country or fighting for one girl's freedom, we'll fight for what's good. Sure, we break a few rules, but guess what? The bad guys, they ain't ever playing by the damn rules. Somebody's got to be the rebels, and ultimately our hearts are in the right place, and our strength stems from our love for one another. That's what makes us a force worth reckoning with, so don't ever, EVER lose sight of that."

Silence as they take in Judge's sincerity.

They all take a deep breath and share apologetic smiles.

"That was really beautiful," says Memphis, wiping her eyes.

Judge hugs Memphis while Spit hugs Taylor and pats her back.

"You should really go into team building," says Spit, "I'm sorry, you guys."

"I'm sorry too," admits Taylor, "Judge, please still be my lawyer if we fuck this up."

A little later, with The Huey now wheeled out of the barn, the engines whine up to speed, and the blades chop through the air, strobing against the midday sun, the Gatling gun mostly duct-taped underneath.

Memphis checks gauges and flicks switches, a makeshift trigger button taped to her control stick.

Spit readies her M15.

Taylor slings the rocket launcher over her shoulder.

Judge grins to herself and says, "You know, for what's supposed to be a break, this sure feels like my day job."

Memphis grabs the control stick. "Ain't no rest for the wicked, right?" She states.

Taylor loads a rocket into the launcher and comments, "The only thing we're missing is helmets."

Spit cocks her rifle. "At least you got no brains to splatter over us," she jokes.

They all exchange amused smiles.

Memphis kisses her hand and taps the Pink Power Ranger.

The engine roars louder, the rotors whir faster, and they lift off, ready for action.

Chapter 4

The girls sit pensively, hair whipping in the breeze, the jet turbine of the Heuy howling and the main rotor thumping as they soar over through the mountains.

They narrow their eyes, ready for battle as they approach the Mine Town fast.

Pancho stands ready with all his Thugs.

A faint rumbling grows louder and louder.

Pancho turns to his gang and shouts, "These bitches think they are so tough! We will show them what is really tough, yeah?"

The Thugs cheer in unison.

Hector stares into the sky, worried, and comments, "I don't like the sound of this."

The Huey cackles around the mountainside.

The Thugs flee to defensive positions, gawking up shocked as it storms over them.

The Girls give them the finger. Here we go!

"There! By the bar!" Calls out Spit.

Thugs drag the kidnapped Girl into the Bar.

The Huey makes a pass.

BANG! BANG! Thugs fire up.

RATATATATATAT! Taylor and Spit fire back with their assault rifles, taking people out.

The Huey swings around, and more Thugs take hits.

Memphis deviously grins as she spots The Skanks, who burned her truck, sprinting up the middle of the road.

The Huey looms in behind them.

CHACHACHACHA! The Skanks disintegrate like beetroots in a blender.

"Seriously, nothin' personal," jokes Memphis.

"Okay, put us down!" Orders Judge.

The Huey lands.

Judge and Taylor bailout.

Spit covers them with suppressive fire as they run to the Bar

Judge and Taylor burst in. BANG BANG! They take out Thugs and race toward a back room where they can hear someone shouting, "Jamás me llevarán vivo!"

They run into the room and freeze.

A Thug with his arm around The Girl and his gun to her head.

"You back off perras," he threatens, "or I kill her! Comprende?"

Taylor sprints back out of the room.

Footsteps close in from elsewhere, confusing the Thug, who glances to one side.

CRASH! Taylor smashes back in through a plaster side wall and puts her gun right against the Thug's head.

BANG! Blood and brains splatter across the room.

"Adios asshole!" Quips Taylor.

The Girl gazes up at her in amazement.

"Hey, it's okay," Judge reassures The Girl, "You speak English? Habla inglés?"

"A little," replies The Girl.

"That's all you gonna need, honey," states Judge, "We're the good guys, okay? Come on."

They run for the entrance, but Thugs run up outside.

"No chance!" Shouts Taylor, "The roof!"

The Huey sweeps over.

BANG! BANG! BANG! A Thug shoots at it.

The Huey soars over him. RATATATAT!

His head pops like a water balloon.

Judge, Taylor, and The Girl burst out onto the roof.

Taylor aims the rocket launcher at Thugs on the ground and fires. WOOOOSH! BOOOOM!

She watches Thugs flee and punches the air triumphantly.

"Chupa mi polla!" Shouts Taylor, *(Translation: 'Suck my Dick.')*

Taylor smiles down at The Girl, thinking she's super cool.

"Eso explica muchas cosas." Exclaims The Girl, *(Translation: 'That explains a lot!')*

RATATATATA! Gunshots hit around them.

Hector across the street, his assault rifle crackling as he fires. They're pinned in.

Taylor tries to get a shot on Hector, but she can't.

Judge calls into the radio, "We need some cover here!"

"Bringin' the noise!" Replies Memphis.

The Huey sweeps in.

RATATATAT! Hector fires up at it.

The Huey has to duck away and circle.

"I can't get a sight on this, asshole!" Complains Spit.

"I've got an idea!" Announces Memphis.

Taylor and Judge watch the Huey hover over them.

"What the hell is she doing?" Questions Judge.

The Huey drops behind the bar.

Judge's eyes widen. "Oh god, no!" She exclaims.

"Umm, you might want to like, keep your heads down," warns Memphis.

The Gatling gun spins up. CHACHACHACHA!

Huge rounds punch into the back of the building.

CHACHACHACHA! Those same rounds smash out the front windows and burst through walls.

Taylor and Judge cover The Girl as rounds tear through

the structure below.

CHACHACHACHA! Hector cowers as rounds hit around him.

He's outta there. He sprints away. CHACHACHACHA! BOOM! A vehicle explodes behind him.

Taylor, Judge, and The Girl stare at the boiling red fireball as the Huey hovers through the black smoke.

They go to climb in but--

Pancho, hidden in a building, with an assault rifle. He carefully aims for the Huey's engine and fires. BANG!

BEEP! BEEP! BEEP! BEEP! Alarms ring out in the Huey.

Memphis cringes. She fights with the control stick and tries to fire.

Nothing. Gun jam.

The Huey hovers away and swings around, out of control.

Taylor and Judge wince, confused.

"This another one of her plans?" Questions Taylor.

Memphis wrestles desperately with the controls while being thrown around in her seat.

WHOOP! WHOOP! WHOOP! WHOOP! More alarms wail.

Spit clutches on for her life, the scenery outside a blur.

The Huey swings completely out of control as smoke pours from an engine.

It hovers over a Mine Shaft, kicks upward, and spins into a death spiral.

Taylor and Judge watch, horrified.

Memphis frantically glances around and grits her teeth. "This landing might suck!" She warns.

Spit's eye bulge. She braces for impact.

CRAAAAAASH! The Huey smashes straight through the wooden head-frame and disappears into the Mine Shaft.

"Oh, hell no!" Cries Judge, staring horrified.

Taylor, Judge, and The Girl race down from the roof.

They burst out of the Bar and sprint toward the wreck,

engaging in gunfire.

RATATATATATATATA! CLICK! They run out of ammo.

They turn back and run to an old Hoist House as shots ping against it, dive inside, and take up defensive positions.

The crashed Huey hangs nose first in the dark mineshaft.

Spit comes to inside it and gazes around.

The cockpit empty, a hole in the windshield, and a bottomless black pit below.

"Memphis?" Yells Spit.

"I'm okay!" Calls back Memphis from a distance.

"What the hell happened?" Asks Spit.

Memphis hangs from a wooden beam below, "Umm... we got shafted. Well, this situation couldn't get any worse!"

The engine on the Huey catches fire, causing the shaft to illuminate.

Spit carefully clambers down the Huey to the shaft.

"I'm coming down," informs Spit, "We'll climb to the bottom."

She eases her way down the cockpit to an open door.

"Wait!" Cries out Memphis, "Bring Kimberly!"

"Kimberly?" Questions Spit.

"On the dashboard!" Replies Memphis.

Spit looks to the dashboard. The Pink Power Ranger. She grabs it and sighs, "A la orden!"

Memphis clambers down the beams of the shaft a little.

Fire drips by her, and she looks down.

Fuel at the base of the shaft, now setting fire to the timber beams.

"Umm, okay," worries Memphis, "now things couldn't get any worse!"

"Stop sayin' that!" Barks Spit, "You're jin-"

BANG! The Gatling gun still attached to the Huey cycles a round and chops into the beam Memphis is hanging from.

"You see!" Shouts Spit.

CHACHACHACHA! The Gatling gun chops the beam in two, causing Memphis to fall and scream.

She crashes through a rotten beam and manages to grab hold of another.

"Well," she concludes with a wince, "I think it's safe to say now it couldn't get any worse! Okay?"

CRACK! The Huey jolts and starts to slip down the shaft.

Spit glares down at her and hisses, "Just shut your stupid mouth!" Before continuing to clamber down beams.

CHACHACHACHA! The gatling gun fires.

Spit freezes.

Memphis falls, crashes against the corner of the shaft, and manages to land upright and balanced on a couple of beams.

She tenderly looks down at the furious fire below.

She looks across to see an old drift shaft.

"There's a way out!" Exclaims Memphis, "quick!"

CREAK. CRACK.

They look up. The Huey slips.

"Hurry!" Screams Memphis.

Spit frantically clambers down.

The Huey drops behind her.

Fire climbs beams below.

She slips and falls, but Memphis catches her as she passes.

CHACHACHACHA! The gatling gun fires.

Spit screams as Memphis heaves her up, bullets whipping past her legs.

The Huey falls.

They run for their lives down the drift shaft as The Huey crashes by, hits the bottom of the main shaft, and BOOOOM! It explodes.

A fireball rushes up the shaft. They hit the deck.

WOOOOOSH! Fire flashes over them and fades out into smoke as they lie panting.

Spit hands over the Pink Power Ranger to Memphis.

"Why do you have to care so much about that thing?" She

asks.

Memphis scoffs, "Because it's like, for good luck, obviously."

From within the confines of the Hoist House, Judge, Taylor and The Girl watch the fireball erupt from the mineshaft.

They stare horrified.

"Memphis, Spit," Judge calls into the radio, "you copy?"

Taylor's eyes glisten, and her jaw quivers as nothing but silence comes back.

"Girls, do you copy?" Urges Judge, "Please!"

Judge turns to Taylor, welling up.

Taylor stares back vengefully, she's already done grieving.

Footsteps approaching.

Taylor tosses down her empty rifle and yanks an old rusty pick axe from the wall.

"Okay," advises Judge, warily, "don't do anything stupid now, girl. Just put a lid on, okay? Put a damn lid on."

Judge cowers and protects The Girl as Taylor puts on a miner's helmet and pounds it with her fist. DONK!

She walks into the next room.

BANG! The helmet is shot straight off her head.

She ducks behind pipes as shots ping behind her.

A Thug waits for her to pop up.

The axe swipes from under the pipes and severs his foot clean off.

YEARGH! He goes down screaming.

Taylor crawls out, grabs his gun off him, pops back up, and aims for the other approaching Thugs

BANG! CLICK! Her ammo already out.

BANG! She ducks as shots zip by her.

She grabs the axe and hurls it at a Thug.

THWACK! It wedges in his collar bone, and he flails around screaming.

The other Thug fires.

She runs at him, holding up the helmet as shots hit it. PING! PING! PING! PING! PING!

"Not what I meant!" Calls out Judge, "Not what I meant!"

CLICK! CLICK! CLICK! The Thug's out.

CRACK! Taylor smacks him out cold with the helmet.

CLICK! A cocking hammer.

Another Thug enters.

Taylor frisbees the helmet across the room.

SMACK! The rusty metal lip impales in his face.

The Girl watches, amazed.

Now someway down the drift shaft, Memphis and Spit walk with flaming pieces of wood in hand.

"Where the hell are we going?" Wonders Spit, "This will just be a dead end, surely?"

Memphis finds an old rope-pulley-style lift cage.

She yanks at the rope, smarks back at Spit, and asks, "How's your tugging technique?"

Spit is unamused.

Back in the Hoist House, the Thug with the pick axe in his collarbone staggers around screaming in pain.

Taylor yanks it out. He collapses.

"Taylor!" Warns Judge, "Look out!"

Another Thug with a gun, right behind Taylor.

She spins around with the axe and takes his forearm clean off.

He clutches his splintered elbow and howls. YEAAARGH!

"Heigh-Ho, dickless!" Shouts Taylor as she tries to pull the gun from the severed hand that's still clutching it.

"Taylor!" Shouts Judge.

SMACK! Taylor takes a punch to the head from the one remaining Thug. A real big remorseless-looking fucker too.

She scrabbles away up a huge hoist pulley, but he grabs her legs.

She thuds to the floor, kicks him in the shin, and climbs the pulley again.

He grabs the gun from the severed hand and turns to fire.

THWACK! She kicks it out of his hands, and it wedges in the hoist gears.

He elbows her legs from under her and climbs up onto the pulley, where they square up to one another.

The Thug growls, "Why don't you get back to your cleaning, bitch."

"Oh, I'm nearly done sweeping up in here," smirks Taylor, "You think you can take out the trash?"

They swing for one another, duck punches, and take hits.

Memphis and Spit pull the lift cage to the top of its shaft and gaze around inside what seems like a cave.

Light beams through the gaps of the boarded-up entrance.

Spit crosses to it and kicks a board away.

The beam of sunlight illuminates something by Memphis, who looks around at a cover draped over something big.

Memphis sweeps it away, and her jaw drops.

A dusty old Dodge Charger that's been stored for decades.

"Are you freaking kidding me!" Exclaims Memphis, "This is a classic! Why would somebody leave this here?"

"Umm, maybe because of this?" Replies Spit as she kicks away more boards.

Memphis crosses to the entrance beside Spit, and her jaw drops as she peers down.

The hillside mined away below them, a near vertical drop for over a hundred feet to the Mine Town.

Spit grabs her radio and calls out, "Judge? Taylor? You out there?"

From within the Hoist House, Judge's eyes bulge as she grabs her radio. "Spit? That you, girl?" She replies, "You with Memphis?"

"Yeah", confirms Spit, "we're okay. You?"

"Oh, we're in a world of trouble," reports Judge, "We need evac right away. You think you can find some transport?"

Spit looks back at The Charger and winces. "Yeah, we already got some... kinda."

"You kidding me, girl?" Exclaims Judge,

Judge looks to the Boiler House from a window.

"You see the building with the big ass chimneys on it?" She asks Spit, "We'll meet you there, okay?"

Spit peers down at the Boiler House in the distance. "See you there. Over and out," she replies.

Judge puts the radio away and wipes away her tears before turning back to see the Thug kick Taylor off the pulley.

BANG! Taylor crashes to the floor.

He takes his gun, one of his feet resting on the big metal hoist gears, and aims at Taylor.

"Hey, sucker!" Calls out Judge with her hand on the brake lever, "Looks like you need a break!"

With a smirk, Judge releases the pulley brake. He freezes.

The gears creak a little. Nothing happens. The gun still wedged in them.

Judge winces. He aims for her instead.

Then suddenly, The Girl calls out, "Chupa verga un burro!"

They all turn to see The Girl by a taut steel pully cable with an axe.

She swings hard at the cable. CRACK! The Thug's eyes bulge.

The cable whips back and bisects him right up the middle, squirting blood over Taylor.

"Woah! Holly fuckin' Jesus!" Taylor exclaims as both sides of his body peel down to the ground.

Taylor stares at The Girl standing proudly with her axe.

The Girl winks back. Taylor wipes blood off herself and nods approvingly.

"C'mon, we're moving," advises Judge, "Spit and Memphis are coming in hot."

Taylor grabs the pistol from the floor, and they run out of the room as maimed Thugs scream and writhe.

Spit winces down at the mine town as Memphis crosses to the Charger and drags away the rest of the covers.

"Are you serious?" Asks Spit.

"Look I'm a pilot," states Memphis, "I can fly anything like, even a car."

"Yeah, well, how'd you think you'll start it, eh? You don't think the battery will be flat, no?"

"Easy. We bump start it."

"Bump start it?"

"Backwards."

"Backwards?"

Memphis tries the door handle, but it won't budge.

She grits her teeth, kicks out the window, and slides in.

"We doin' this?" She asks Spit.

A Dodge Charger, a girl dressed as Daisy Duke, a plan to jump out a mineshaft, fuck yeah we are!

Spit smashes the other window and slips inside.

"See, no keys?" Points out Spit.

"Give me your knife." Says Memphis.

Spit hands over her flick knife.

Memphis slices off the barrel, rams it into the ignition, and clicks it around.

"Where'd you learn that?" asks Spit, somewhat impressed.

"Try running away from home a few dozen times," replies Memphis as she clutches the wheel and grabs the shifter. "Hold on to your... No, wait."

She pulls out the Pink Power Ranger, sticks it on the dash, kisses her hand, and pats it.

"Oh yeah," sighs Spit, "our real lucky charm."

"Okay, here goes," announces Memphis.

She releases the parking brake, and they roll back as Memphis pumps the clutch and tries to select reverse.

The gears grind. The speed increases.

"Come on, quickly!" Urges Spit.

Memphis fights with the stick and gets it into reverse.

She tries the ignition. They jolt. Nothing.

Beams whip by fast.

Spit looks out the rear window, worried. "Come on! Ándale!"

Memphis tries again. They jolt. Nothing.

She grits her teeth and tries once more.

VROOM! The Charger barks into life.

She hits the brakes hard, but the tyres skid on loose gravel.

Spit watches the end of the shaft approach fast.

"Stop, stop, stop, stop, stop!" She cries as they keep sliding.

They wince, not slowing until they crash through beams and SCRUNCH. They stop at the last moment.

Spit sighs with relief.

"Seriously, I've got this," assures Memphis, "Now, strap in. We're cleared for takeoff."

She smugly smiles, grabs a gear, and floors it.

ZZZZZZZZZZZZ! They don't move at all.

Memphis looks out her window to find they're stuck in wet sludge.

"Oh, I see you real got this," mocks Spit.

Memphis looks back, embarrassed.

Judge, Taylor and The Girl burst into the Boiler House to find it full of lab gear. A rack of a dozen microwaves and barrels of chemicals strewn about.

"I guess this is what you need when half your gang only eats burritos," comments Taylor.

"Oh they cooking, that's for sure," confirms Judge, "This whole setup, it all makes sense. These guys aren't into some two-bit grand theft auto bullshit."

Taylor peers up at an old cabinet on which a large *EXPLOSIVES* warning sign hangs from the front. She smiles coyly.

Judge studies the lab gear in more detail. "No, this is some serious drug production shit," she comments, "That's what this is, a goddamn crack factory."

"Crack factory? Oh man, that'd be a great name for a strip club." Jokes Taylor, "Hey, check this out!"

Judge looks around to find Taylor proudly waving two old sticks of dynamite.

Judge freezes, terrified, and slowly urges, "Girl, you got to stop waving those things around, okay?"

Taylor sees the terror in Judge's eyes and freezes.

"That's dynamite," continues Judge, backing away slowly, "You know what that does when it's stored for a real long time?"

"No!" Replies Taylor, her eyes growing wider, "What is this? Mythbusters?"

"It sweats, okay?" Explains Judge, "It sweats pure nitroglycerin, and nitroglycerin is some real volatile shit."

Taylor winces and holds the sticks of dynamite like they are, well, sticks of dynamite.

"Well, it's not the only thing sweating now!" Whimpers Taylor.

"Look, just put them down, okay?" Advises Judge, "Carefully, real carefully."

Taylor eeks them into a nearby microwave, and shuts the door as if it will contain any blast.

"Seriously?" Questions Judge, "That's your go-to place to put dynamite?"

Judge thinks for a moment and narrows her eyes.

"What you thinking, Judge?" Asks Taylor.

A smile grows across Judge's face as she looks around at the place and replies, "I think I'm having what you might call a lightbulb moment."

Back in the Mine Tunnel, Memphis stares back at the spinning wheels failing to find any traction. She grits her teeth and guns the engine hard. ZZZZZZZZZZZZZZZZ!

Spit pushes as hard as she can, her heels deep in sludge. "Argh! Easy! Easy!" She shouts.

The Charger slithers out the sludge.

"Wow," exclaims Memphis, "you're a lot stronger than-"

She turns to find Spit pissed off and covered in dirt.

"This better be worth it," warns Spit.

The microwaves in the Boiler House now loaded with dynamite.

Judge carefully screws a lightbulb she's removed from a lamp onto the last stick of explosives.

Taylor watches her work and concludes, "Well, I guess we now know how many lawyers it takes to change a lightbulb. One, and it will cost you everything you have."

Spit and Memphis look around worried as creaking and cracking sounds start to fill the Mine Tunnel, the support beams they crashed into now splintering and giving way.

Dirt trickles. Rocks drop.

Spit leaps through the Charger window.

"Go, go, go, go, go!" She yells.

Memphis floors it.

The Charger roars, fires rooster tails, and launches like a scalded cat as the shaft collapses gradually behind it.

Beams flicker by. The entrance starts to close up with dirt, and the light fades.

"Eres Loca!" Screams Spit.

Memphis grabs the next gear, stares ahead intensely, and

shouts, "Don't call me crazy!"

The Charger bursts out shaft in an explosion of dirt.

Thugs in the Mine Town below gaze up amazed.

Suddenly, the whole cliff-side, weakened by the collapsed tunnel, gives way and drops.

The Charger crashes back to Earth and races down the cliff like it's a giant skate ramp, a landslide forming behind it.

"Ay-yi-ai! Faster!" Cries Spit.

"Hang on!" Yells Memphis.

The Charger hurtles toward the town as Thugs desperately flee.

Memphis stares ahead and aims for a collapsed building that looks remarkably ramp-like. They both wince.

The Charger kicks into the air and soars upward, with dirt and dust streaming from the underside and a high-pitched, ear-piercing scream shrieking from within it.

YEEEEEEEEEEEAAAAAAAGGGHIII!!! Spit screams as Memphis stares meanly ahead.

A wave of rubble from the landside follows close behind, ripping through buildings, smashing them to pieces, and crushing all the remaining Thugs, sending blood and torn-off limbs everywhere.

The landslide settles, and the screaming gets louder.

CRASH! The Charger touches down and roars away to the Boiler House, where it growls up and skids around in a cloud of dust.

"Quick!" Spit urges with a beaming smile, "Do the horn thing!"

Memphis slams the horn.

FAAAAARRP. They frown.

Inside the Boiler House, Taylor, Judge, and The Girl crouch hidden behind a table.

Judge threads a very long stick slowly forward.

It prods a microwave timer button over and over.

"C'mon, just how much time will this need?" Asks Taylor.

"Oh, I'm nuking this shit," replies Judge.

Judge positions the stick over the start button.

"You ready?" She asks.

Taylor and The Girl tentatively nod and get ready to run.

Judge winces and prods the button.

They bolt.

The microwave hums, and the bulb flickers.

Taylor, Judge, and The Girl sprint out while Memphis and Spit wait by the Charger.

Taylor reaches for the door.

"No, they don't work!" Insists Memphis, You have to get in through the-"

Taylor yanks the door open with no problem and throws The Girl into the back seat.

Taylor glares at Memphis and clips her around the ear.

"No Dukes of Hazard!" Taylor barks, "A-Team only!"

Memphis and Taylor fight back and forth with the door.

"Where the hell, you guys, been?" Asks Judge.

Spit looks back offended, clothes filthy and the dust still settling from the landslide behind her.

"We just jumped a car outta mountain!" Exclaims Spit, "We're crazy! What've you guys managed to do?

Taylor and Judge look at each other and look back at the Boiler House.

Inside, the bulb in the microwave flickers like crazy. BOOM! It blows.

BOOM! BOOM! BOOM! BOOM! Each microwave explodes in sequence.

BOOM! The explosives cabinet explodes.

BOOM! BANG! BANG! BOOM! BANG! The barrels explode.

BOOOOOOOOOOOOOOOOOOOOOOOOOOOOOOOM! The whole building goes up in a monumental explosion that sends debris for miles around.

"That!" Announces Taylor, "That's the shit we're accomplishing!"

They all stare up at the mammoth fireball climbing into the sky.

"Shaboom!" Shouts Judge, "Stick that up your nose and snort it, you jive crack peddling turkeys!"

Taylor and Judge smack in a triumphant high-five.

"Who... who are you people?" Asks The Girl from the safety of the back seat.

"We're Hell's Belles, honey," explains Judge, "and this dumb shit is our speciality. Now let's get your little brown Mexican ass back to your mother."

They climb in the Charger.

It slews around and roars away.

With scenery blowing by and the engine roaring, Spit looks at The Girl and checks a graze on her cheek.

"Estás bien?" Spit asks, *(Translation: 'Are you alright?')*

"Si! Este hombre y su esposa negra son bastante los luchadores!" Replies The Girl with a keen smile, *(Translation: 'Yes! This handsome man and his black wife are quite the fighters!')*

Spit looks at Taylor, who smiles smugly back.

"Looks like somebody's a role model," boasts Taylor with no idea what The Girl has actually said.

The Charger races along an empty access road, seemingly with a clear path to victory, but the Tow Truck slowly rises up beside them, racing alongside on a parallel track, thick black smoke pouring from the stacks.

It swerves in behind and rams the Charger.

Hector grins down menacingly from behind the wheel.

"Get us away from that thing!" Orders Judge.

Memphis fights with the wheel. "Wow! Great idea,

Judge!" She shouts back, sarcastically.

The Charger swerves. The Truck keeps up.

Spit points ahead and calls out, "Look!"

An old gatehouse. The only way through a small Dodge Charger sized gap.

They smile.

Memphis aims carefully, threading the wheel, and The Charger only just slips through with splinters showering from the fenders.

The girls look back and grin, but--

The Tow Truck smashes through the whole gatehouse, shattering the timber like matchsticks.

They frown.

The Tow Truck closes right in, the menacing grille looming over them.

"Memphis," pleads Judge, "do something, girl!"

Memphis stares back, worried, and asks, "Even something a little crazy?"

"Girl, crazy is all we've got left!"

"Okay then…"

Memphis takes a deep breath and cries, "BELLE BREAK!"

Everyone else looks at each other, confused.

Memphis cuts the wheel hard.

The Charger swerves onto the dirt, spins around, and slews back into the road sideways, clipping the front of Tow Truck before spinning against it, smashing the cab hard, and pirouetting gradually to a halt.

The Tow Truck growls to a stop in the distance as The Girls sit shaken.

"What the hell was that, Memphis!" Yells Judge, "Crashing? Crashing was your plan? Have you finally fuckin' lost it?"

They watch Hector drop out of the Tow Truck with his machine gun, a delighted grin across his face.

"Oh hell," worries Judge, "anybody else got ammo?"

"A little," hopes Taylor.

"Get us out of here, Memphis," orders Judge.

"Wait!" Demands Memphis.

SNAP! The cigarette lighter pops out, red hot and ready for action.

Memphis grabs it, hurls it as hard as she can out the window, and-

WOOOOOMP! Fresh fuel in the road ignites.

Flames charge toward the Tow Truck and-

Hector looks back at the truck to see the fuel tank destroyed in the crash and a trail of gas right between his legs.

His eyes bulge. WOOMPH! He goes up in a huge fireball along with the Tow Truck.

Everyone but Memphis looks on in shock.

"Who's burnin' who's truck now, fucknuts!" Shouts Memphis.

The Charger roars away and passes the burning wreck, but Hector runs out of the flames howling and throws himself onto the hood, his whole body on fire.

The Girls all scream and duck as he clambers onto the roof, his arms flailing through the side windows.

He manages to grab Spit and drags her out of the window.

"Memphis, stop!" Cries Judge.

Memphis hits the brakes.

BANG! They don't slow down and look back.

Pancho right behind them in the Firebird, pushing them along.

BANG! BANG! Judge and Taylor lean out the windows and try to take him out with the little ammo they have.

Spit tries to fend off burning Hector on the roof.

He pins her on her back and clutches her neck tight, glaring as his skin sears and blisters.

Spit manages to get her long muscular leg right back under him

KICK! Her filthy heel punches through his eye.

He screams, writhing. She winces as she can't get it back out of his socket.

KICK! She spikes a heel through the other eye.

He desperately flails, face attached to her feet.

She turns him around, coils, and kicks him off the back of the Charger.

He wedges under the nose of the Firebird and slows it down, allowing the Charger to race away as Spit slips back inside.

Pancho has to stop the Firebird to get around Hector's body.

"You stupid mamon fucker!" He growls.

The Charger tears down the road.

The Firebird storms after and closes in.

Memphis keeps the pedal to the metal while checking the mirror. "We're not gonna lose this guy!" She warns,

"Just get us back to base, okay!" Urges Judge.

A bend approaches. They wince and hold on.

Memphis cuts the wheel, and The Charger slews around the bend, all the tyres screeching.

It suddenly breaks into a drift.

Memphis keeps her cool, carefully easing the wheel back and forth, and controls the slide.

The Charger squirms from side to side and roars up the road.

Spit, Taylor, and The Girl look out the rear window to watch the shadowy black Firebird racing into the bend.

Pancho winces and aggressively fights with the wheel.

The Firebird screeches around the bend, oversteers, clips a bush and loses speed.

Spit smiles and proudly pats Memphis on the shoulder.

"Stay cool," she urges, "You're losing him!"

The Diner approaches.

Memphis reaches for the handbrake and screams, "HOLD

ONTO YOUR TITS!"

The back wheels of the Charger lock up and billow smoke.

It kicks sideways and skids into the car lot of The Diner, throwing up a cloud of dust as it comes to a halt.

The girls get out, run inside, and shut the door.

The Firebird roars up and grinds to a stop.

Pancho creeps out, grins at the Diner, and raises his AK as the dust slowly settles.

"Come out, little pigs," he sings before checking around, "Don't make me come in there after you."

He slowly skulks forward. "You're fucked, okay?" he goads, "So why don't you bitches come out."

Silence. He waits a few moments and spits on the ground. "Face me like the men that you wish you were, eh?" he demands.

Clicking. Arming. Cocking.

The Customers pop up at the windows with all their weapons raised.

He goes to fire.

BANG! BANG! POP! BOOM! POP! BANG! BANG! BOOM! POP! BANG! Gratuitous gunfire from everyone wielding everything from shotguns to revolvers to blowback pistols. No mercy.

He goes limp, stares back with horror in his eyes, and drops to the dirt, lying gasping, somehow still alive but riddled with bullets and completely fucked.

Crunching footsteps grow louder, a shadow slowly casts over him, and a rifle barrel lowers to his head.

He looks up to see The Girl staring back down the sights, right into his pleading eyes.

"Adiós asshole," she says with a mean tone.

BANG! She puts one right through his nugget.

Taylor clutches her mouth. Her eyes well up.

"Oh my god," she whimpers, "I taught her that. She's one

of us now."

The Girl stands there, shaking with vengeance, as Mrs Martinez runs in and embraces her tightly.

They cry tears of happiness, causing The girls to well up too, Taylor the worst.

"You gotta love it when a family comes back together," sniffs Judge.

"Eso me encanta, es hermoso," croaks Spit.

Memphis wipes her eyes and looks to Taylor. "What's the matter, Taylor?" she asks, "You like, actually getting broody now?"

Taylor pathetically nods.

She crosses to The Girl, takes a knee, and presents her M15.

"I know this rifle's got no bullets," she explains, "and that piece of shit Knight Rider car's like, thirty years old, but I want you to take them, okay? Take them and protect these pussies in this diner. I'm so, so proud of you."

Taylor ceremoniously hands over the M15, which The Girl proudly receives.

"Eres el padre que nunca tuve," announces The Girl, *(Translation: 'You are the father I never had.')*

Taylor strokes her hair adoringly and smiles. "I don't know what that means," she admits, "but to me it was beautiful."

Taylor hugs The Girl. Everyone else also lovingly embraces one another while Lily, the dog, licks blood off dead Pancho's face.

As the sun makes its way back toward the horizon, The Girls all sit ready to leave in The Charger, Memphis and Judge in the front, Taylor and Spit in the back, with everyone standing proudly around them.

Bill crouches beside Judge's window.

"So what's next for you girls?" He asks.

Judge goes to reply, but her phone rings.

She checks it as The Girls all exchange looks and declines the call.

"Let's just say, we're currently pursuing career options," she replies.

"Well, if you're ever passing by, it's on the house, okay?" Offers Bill.

"Hell, Bill, technically, that would still be extortion," she jokes.

"C'mon, drop by sometime," he urges, "Give a guy a chance to prove himself."

Bill shoots her a flirtatious smile, and she shoots one back.

Mr Martinez and The Girl cross over to Taylor.

The Girl grins up at her new mentor with undying admiration.

"Que tus cojones crecer fuerte con la derrota de nuestro enemigo," she wishes Taylor, *(Translation: 'May your balls grow strong with the defeat of our nemesis.')*

Taylor awkwardly smiles back, leans to Spit, and asks, "What did she say?"

Spit goes to mock but pauses and thinks better of it.

"She says," translates Spit, contemplating what to say for a moment, "You have the prettiest eyes in the world."

Taylor wells up again and whispers something back into Spit's ear.

Spit turns to the Girl. "Ella dice eres las estrellas en sus ojos," she repeats, *(Translation: 'You are the stars in her eyes.')*

The Girl grips the M15 and salutes Taylor, who starts weeping hopelessly.

"What the hell is happening to me?" She sobs.

Memphis shakes her head, puts the Charger in gear, and quips, "To think people have the gall to say we're a bad influence."

The Girls look back at everyone.

"You people just remember," advises Judge, "when there's

trouble around and nobody's man enough to step up and do something about it, Hell's Belles might just be coming to town."

The Charger wheel spins away, and everyone waves while wiping dirt out of their eyes.

The Girl stands meanly by the Firebird and shakes her M15 at the wide-eyed customers.

"Todo lo que usted bitches trabajo para mí ahora!" She barks, *(Translation: 'All you bitches work for me now!')*

Mrs Martinez hurries over and smacks her with her shoe, before snatching the rifle out of her hands.

The Charger races up the long, empty highway, with the chrome gleaming in the setting sun and the mountains on the horizon basking in a golden hue.

"So guys, seriously," questions Memphis, "like, where are we actually going?"

"Okay, I got this," assures Judge, "The sun sets in west, right?"

"Judge, if you don't know, then I should definitely ride up front," argues Taylor.

"Ay-yi-ai, girls, please!" Exclaims Spit, "I think I need to pee again already."

THE END

Printed in Great Britain
by Amazon